FINDING MR. BRIGHTSIDE

FINDING MR. BRIGHTSIDE

JAY CLARK

Christy Ottaviano Books
Henry Holt and Company
New York

Henry Holt and Company, LLC
Publishers since 1866
175 Fifth Avenue
New York, New York 10010
macteenbooks.com

Library of Congress Cataloging-in-Publication Data
Clark, Jay (Jay Patrick), 1982–
Finding Mr. Brightside / Jay Clark.—First edition.
pages cm
Summary: Abram and Juliette have lived down the street from each other all their lives but had no connection until Juliette's mother and Abram's father had an affair that ended in a deadly car crash. Then a year later, the teens begin a tentative relationship while picking up their prescription medications.
ISBN 978-0-8050-9257-8 (hardback)—ISBN 978-1-250-07365-5 (trade paperback)—
ISBN 978-0-8050-9638-5 (e-book)
[1. Dating (Social customs)—Fiction. 2. Neighborhoods—Fiction. 3. Loss (Psychology)—Fiction. 4. Drug abuse—Fiction. 5. Single-parent families—Fiction.]
I. Title. II. Title: Finding Mister Brightside.
PZ7.C553553Fin 2015 [Fic]—dc23 2014039994

First Edition—2015 / Designed by Patrick Collins
Printed in the United States of America by
R. R. Donnelley & Sons Company, Harrisonburg, Virginia

1 3 5 7 9 10 8 6 4 2

To my family,
to my girl,
and to anyone who's ever filled a prescription
or fallen in love
(I think that covers everyone)

PROLOGUE

ABRAM

SHE TAKES A CAB every Saturday morning. Not sure where; still want to go, too—I'm up for whatever when it comes to her. Instead, I'm crouching beside my favorite window like the creepy, uninvited neighbor I am, waiting for her to walk outside with a frown on her perfect face. Wouldn't be surprised if my mom's standing behind me with her arms crossed, wondering what's gotten into me.

Hold up. There she is, slamming her front door precisely on time, speed-walking toward the cab, annoyed that everything is making her late. Her hair is down and straight today, not in its usual tightly wound bun contraption. She puts more effort into getting ready on Saturdays than she ever does for school, that boring place we both go where she also pretends I don't exist. Not that I'm blaming her for treating me with silence only—she has her reason, and it's a good one.

As her cab backs out of the driveway and begins speeding down the road toward my house, I crawl to the side, out of view. I like to imagine her heading to a happier place that isn't church, because from what I can tell, home and school don't seem to be providing a barrel of laughs. I bet she manages to be productive on the way, maybe fills out college applications similar to the blank forms collecting dust atop my dresser, only for better colleges, until she starts feeling carsick . . . and then forces herself to complete them in their entirety, anyway. That's how she rolls when she jogs, too, so determined to out-sprint whatever's haunting her. I've come to know this side of her naturally; I'd see her running along the path by the tennis courts where my father and I used to drill pretty much every day, until *that* day.

It's almost like she and I were meant to be complete strangers with an unthinkable tragedy in common.

1

Juliette

THERE SHE IS, standing behind the counter: my CVS pharmacist, Mindy. We're on a first-name basis. Not sure how she feels about that, but the other day I hid inside the Starbucks bathroom for five minutes to avoid running into her, so . . .

I walk up and slide my prescription toward Mindy's waiting hand, ignoring the sign reminding me not to forget this year's flu shot on purpose again.

"Hi, Juliette."

"Hey, Mindy."

Mindy picks up the paper, stares at it like we don't go through the same embarrassing routine every month.

"Let me check if I have this medication in stock."

She does—I called ahead but don't want to admit it, just watch as Mindy walks over to the safe where they keep all the stuff worth getting prescribed. She crouches down and practically folds herself over the front of it, paranoid I might memorize the combo as she punches it in. At best, she looks awkward. At worst, I've already memorized it—never know when things will get more desperate than they already are.

She walks back, tells me they have it, and starts typing my order into the computer. Frowning, she says, "Your insurance won't cover this until the end of the month."

"Really?" I say innocently. Went a little overboard on my daily dosage last week. After hesitating for what seems like an appropriate amount of time, I tell her I'll pay out of pocket and remove my sketchy online discount card from my purse. Mindy shoots me a conflicted expression that I'm not mentally equipped to help her feel better about. I have my own problems, clearly.

"When would you like to pick up *your Adderall?*" she practically bellows.

"Ten minutes, please," I say, my voice a sharp, pointy whisper.

Mindy pushes back the bangs she probably shouldn't have cut in the first place, wanting me to understand how heavy the burden I'm placing on her is. The store is empty. Mindy's going to be okay.

When we're almost finished with each other, a noise rings out from the aisle behind me—a bottle of pills dropping to the floor. We're not as alone as I thought. Nevertheless, I don't turn around. Why? So I can see someone I know? Or, worse, someone-I-know's mom? I look up toward the shoplifters-beware mirror mounted to the corner wall. Not liking what's reflecting back at me. At all.

I'm seeing a crown of wavy blond surfer-dude hair, droopy gray sweatpants, flip-flops. But it's the bewilderingly cute face, *his* face, and the watery-blue color of his eyes, which stir up feelings I haven't yet figured out how to compartmentalize.

For now, I give my brain tips like *Stop it* and *I hate you*. I'm still getting a faceful of Abram Morgan at CVS, on a Friday, at midnight, dropping a bottle of fish oil on the floor.

He places the bottle back on the shelf, mutters an apology to no one in particular, and walks away. Why is he here? Shouldn't he be playing tennis, or doing whatever Abram Morgan does on the weekends so I don't have to worry about seeing the waistband of his boxer briefs outside of eighth-period English?

I finish up with Mindy and then duck past the greeting cards into the most boy-repelling aisle I can find: the tampon section. Then I go one aisle past that one, because I just can't be that girl right now, even in hiding. Eyes lowered as far as they can go, I examine the boxes of hair color as if I'm in the market for a new hue that's destined to result in my best friend, Heidi, a genuinely nice person who could do a lot better for herself than the damaged goods I'm bringing to the table, throwing me a pity party and having to pretend it's just as fun as a regular party.

One of the hair models, a doll-like woman with an intentionally disheveled blond bob, looks eerily similar to my mother. Her lips are painted a deep red, her chin tilts upward like she's found a secret beauty ingredient bubbling forth from the fountain of youth, and wouldn't you like to buy what it is? A chill plays the piano down my spine.

I pick up the box—the last one on the shelf—and drop it

quietly to the floor, sliding it underneath the bottom shelf with my worn-out running shoe. For a second I flash back to my mom in a hospital bed, eyes closed, face flawless and scratch-free, her brain the only injured part of her body. Even close to death, she looked very, very much alive.

My chest feels tight, and I can't breathe, and, new rule, no thinking about my mother on life support again for at least the rest of my days. Especially with Abram Morgan, a living reminder of who she'd become, nearby.

Then it hits me. Not another anxiety attack. Not anything close to inner peace. The Adderall I classily swallowed at the kitchen sink, before my two-mile jog over here? Unfortunately, that's it. The side effects are giving me a false sense of euphoric confidence that I could maybe, possibly, confront Abram Morgan, head-on, and "kill my frog," as my well-meaning father, a lifelong people-procrastinator himself, likes to preach but rarely leaves the house to practice.

Say I did walk over to Abram right now—how would I go about forcing casual conversation? Should I unzip my track jacket so he can get a clearer view of my protruding clavicles? Flirtatiously release my dry-shampooed hair from my extra-taut runner's bun, mid-sentence, to indicate how relaxed I'm not in his presence? Smile through the pain I've been distracting myself from by taking more than my fair share of ADHD pills?

I start searching for him, pretending I'm the silly-but-lovable blond heroine (addict) in a low-budget indie film I just made up. Working title: *Prescription for Love*. My character, a type-A smart girl with mom issues and a one-track mind, is completely unaware she's about to find a cute guy where she least expected, at CVS, while waiting for her refill. *Prescription for Love* has direct-to-DVD flop written all over it, but there's a Redbox conveniently located outside the entrance here, should anyone want to rent it after we're done filming.

There he is, in the candy section: Abram. Deep breath. I'll do my best to make the next scene more take-charge than outtake, but no promises, being that his father killed my mother a year ago.

2

ABRAM

I'm always amazed by what I discover at CVS while waiting for my antidepressant to get refilled. Colored pencils, dog treats, socks that'll improve my blood circulation—all of these items have found a home inside my little red basket.

What I didn't expect to find here tonight, at midnight especially, was Juliette Flynn, completing a transaction at the drop-off counter. I was staring at her, not-really-examining a bottle of burp-less fish oil, when I blew my cover and dropped the bottle. The noise was loud enough to make the pharmacist jump out of her skin, but not Juliette. She looked up into the shoplifter's mirror, saw it was me, flexed her angular cheekbones, and didn't even turn around. The toughest of cookies. I can think of easier things to be consistent about, you know? Eating cookies, for starters—just threw some in my basket and plan on proving that point later with my boys, Ben & Jerry.

Sure, I'm in the market for another friend or two. But

now Juliette's back to avoiding me, so I probably can't befriend her.

At first I get a kick out of watching her pretend to shop for hair dye, lug around that designer purse, hide her face from wherever she thinks I'm lurking—I'm over here, by the tampons. Then I feel the weight of why she's keeping me at arm's length in the first place.

I grab a bag of Reese's Peanut Butter Cups from an end-cap Halloween display and start walking toward the main candy section, in search of a replacement for the Big Red I stole from Mom's secret candy drawer (the secret's out). The gum's on sale . . . but only for customers who remember their ExtraCare cards, which I have never. I'm reaching for the last remaining pack when I see a second hand that's much softer-looking than my own, heading in the same direction.

Juliette. Incredibly close. Her alert green cat-eyes are scratching through my lazy blues, making me feel like I'm in trouble for not doing something I honestly forgot about. Her face bears no blemishes, no freckles, no emotions; just smooth, impenetrable surface. I might have that defensive, survival-mode look on my face, too, if I weighed somewhere in the high nineties. She could use a few more trips to the Taco Bell drive-thru.

"Sorry," she says, pulling her hand back.

"You like Big Red, too?"

"I was getting it for my dad."

"Same," I say. "For my mom, I mean." Except I'm sure the last thing this enigmatic girl wants is for our surviving parents to have something in common, too. I hold out the gum to her. "You go ahead."

She shakes her head. "I'll find something else."

I wait, watch as she selects a box of Hot Tamales and then turns back to me.

"What are those?" Juliette asks, pointing to the circulation socks in my basket. Unclear why I thought they were such a good idea fifteen minutes ago, I hand them over. She takes them, examines the label for a second. "My dad needs these. He never gets out of his swivel chair."

"My kind of guy."

She doesn't smile. I offer her the socks and she accepts, thanks me, and situates them in her left hand with the Hot Tamales. At the same time, the giant purse slung over her right shoulder is looking heavier by the minute.

"Want to put your stuff in my basket until you're ready to pay?"

"Not really."

"Cool."

Her free hand reaches around toward her bun. She contemplates taking her hair down, then decides against it. Then she goes through these motions again and arrives at the same conclusion.

"Sorry, I'm not the best at making conversation," she says.

I act like this is the craziest self-assessment ever—"What? Noooo, you're good"—probably overdoing it.

"You have a dog?" she asks.

"Maybe," I say mysteriously, thinking I've missed something. "Why?"

Juliette points to the dog treats I forgot were in my basket.

"Sorry, yeah. A golden retriever."

Her mood goes from dark to darker before I can do anything about it. I have to hold myself back from making a physical-contact-based gesture that wouldn't be appreciated.

"Something wrong?" I ask.

"Yes, with my dad . . . He doesn't believe in family pets."

I stop myself from mentioning that my dad had a similar policy, one that my mom and I conveniently forgot about on our way to the dog breeder's place.

"That's disappointing," I say.

"Agree." Then Juliette's stomach growls, and I consider offering her a biscuit as a joke, but it wouldn't be funny.

"Hungry?" I say, because I can't help myself.

"Not at all."

I'm amazed by how resolutely she's able to ignore the growl.

"In that case, I think there's an animal living inside you."

Her stomach growls again, louder this time, more like a roar. She still doesn't flinch.

"I was going to stop by Taco Bell after here, if you, uh . . . ?"

The scrunched-up nose she gives me back indicates she has other plans. Then she tells me she's jogging home, and it's my turn to make a scrunchy face.

"Just keep me company for ten minutes," I bargain, minus any chips. "I'm more fascinating the longer you're around me. Promise."

No response.

"Their drive-thru is the fastest in town."

"Okay," she says.

"Okay . . . ?"

"Okay, I'll go to Taco Bell with you for ten minutes."

The speedy-drive-thru angle is what sold her? Both confused and thrilled by her sudden change of heart, I watch as she power-walks toward the prescription pickup area, hoping this is the beginning of something that has a lot more of her in it. I start walking over to join her, but then change my mind, not really wanting Juliette to watch me sign for a big bag of Paxil. Nope, I'll just get it tomorrow.

Waiting outside at the Redbox next to the entrance, I look over to my car and remind myself to drive well below the speed limit. The last thing I need is Juliette worrying I'll take a thirty-five-mph curve going seventy and roll the vehicle three times. Like my dad did that night, a year ago, with Juliette's mom in his passenger seat.

3

Juliette

MY DAD WOULD never approve of my riding in Abram Morgan's SUV, so it's a good thing I have no plans to tell him about it. Abram overcautiously drives through to the fluorescent Taco Bell menu and orders something called a Doritos Locos Supreme. Five of them. I make a bizarre *yum* noise and tell him I'll have what he's having, sounding like a foreign exchange student.

I offer to pay as Abram pulls up to the window, but he insists. I insist back, telling him I have this thing about not owing people money. (Just don't want to owe him anything.)

"I get it," he says, finally accepting my card. "I keep forgetting to take my wallet to school, and I owe two or three people lunch money right now—not a good way to live."

He doesn't get it, but it's considerate of him to downplay my issue by bringing up one of his. I should say something nice about him in return.

"I like your heated seats."

"Thanks," he says, smiling.

Abram still hands the cashier his card. I can't protest because I'm attempting to dry-swallow a pill chunk (I like to break my two-pills-per-day dosage into quarters under the delusion I'm taking more). I manage to cough it down, smiling innocently as he looks over and asks if I'm okay. Thinking the smile is for him, the cashier gives me a perverted look like he knows his way around a taco. Please make it stop. Abram asks for extra packets of mild sauce and drives away.

Look at Abram Morgan behind the wheel, sunroof open, wind in his hair, an overstuffed sack of questionably Mexican food between his legs. Okay, enough. I'm not going to be the girl who pulls him up by the straps of his flip-flops, prunes his scraggly sideburns with a nose-hair trimmer, and transforms him into four-year-college material.

But I'll admit that there's a hopelessly endearing quality to him. And coexisting with someone else who's halfway to orphanhood definitely takes the pressure off. Neither of us feels like we have to give the other a bouquet of daisies just for getting out of bed and taking things one pill at a time.

"Why didn't you pick up your Paxil at CVS?" Rude of me to ask this right as he's taking his first bite.

He doesn't seem fazed, just resumes the bite while making a noise that sounds like a question mark.

"Sorry, I saw a bag of pills next to mine with your name on it."

"S'okay," he says, swallowing. "Honestly? I was embarrassed. Thought you'd think I was weird for being on an antidepressant."

I raise an eyebrow and point to the prescription bag sticking out of my purse.

"Your doctor put you on one, too?" Abram asks.

"I'm sure he would have if I hadn't faked my ADHD symptoms."

Abram thinks I'm joking and laughs, saying, "Crazy how quick they are to prescribe meds these days, you know? I've never been able to tell if mine are working."

"So why take them?"

"Hmm," he says, "habit?"

A few tacos later, Abram is pulling up the driveway of my house before I can tell him to park anywhere else. The blinds covering my dad's office window remain in place.

"I don't feel like going in there," I say, reaching for my purse.

"Then come over to my house," Abram offers. "My mom is at the casino with my aunt. They're winning right now, so it could be a while." He hands me his phone so I can see a picture of his mom—an attractive, harmless-looking blond with buxom to spare—bending down beside a slot machine and smiling. "She's pretty," I say, relieved that it's true. Abram smiles. I can tell he's proud of her, worries over her, loves her . . . mostly because I'm reading some of their texts right now. Lots of tech-support questions from her about her iPad and patient responses from him.

"Give me two minutes to lie to my dad," I say, handing back his phone.

"Take your time."

• • •

I find my father hiding from the world in his cluttered den, sitting at his desk reading several opened books at once. Ben Flynn is a full-time novelist who's been working on his first book for the last twenty years, thanks to a large trust fund he inherited from his grandfather. Considering I've permanently borrowed his credit card, I'm not one to judge. Tonight he's dressed in his favorite flannel shirt and sweatpants, his hair sticking out in Einstein-inspired tufts. A mug of thick, black coffee sits cold in front of him; that's actually how he likes it. Don't touch his papers! There are passwords written all over them, and he gets nervous.

I wish he'd let me burn down that old dollhouse perched on the table behind him. It's his real-life inspiration for how the serial-killer character in his book plotted his murders, right down to the last ketchup-blood stain and overturned piece of mini furniture. If Dad ever finishes *The Dollhouse Killer*, no one will publish it because it's basically a rip-off of this one *CSI* episode that he doesn't remember watching and I don't have the heart to remind him he's seen.

Careful not to disturb his rhythm, I set the box of Hot Tamales next to his coffee. He looks up from his book and does his best to turn up the corners of his lips. I do the same, re-creating his pain; it's only fair. *Hi, Dad.*

"Get yourself some new socks?" he asks, popping a Hot Tamale into his mouth and pointing to the pair in my hands.

"They're for you," I say, placing them on his desk. He reaches out and runs his fingers along the circulation-improvement material, his sleep-deprived eyes full of gratitude he can't express without stumbling over his words.

"How's the writing coming?" I ask.

"Technical difficulties," he says, pointing to the blue error screen of his 1990s computer. My eyes roll over to the unopened MacBook Pro box leaning against the wall next to his desk. Mom's gift to him two Christmases ago. Even as she was avoiding him, or screwing him over, which I believe she was at that time, Mom kept trying to help my dad stop being his own worst enemy. He hated the laptop, and she knew he would, but she still took the risk. I always admired her fearlessness. In contrast, what did I get him that year? The safe bet: socks and an ink cartridge for his equally ancient printer. He loved them.

"I'm going back out for a few minutes," I say. "Heidi's having lady problems."

Dad shudders and peeks out the window. "You sure that's her car?"

"What?"

"Doesn't Heidi drive a white Volvo with expired license plates?"

"Impounded. That's her mom's car."

He takes off his reading glasses, his gaze steady and full of skepticism. "Or is it the Morgan boy's?"

I shrug like it could be his car, too, wondering why I didn't tell Abram I'd meet him at his house.

"What's the point of this, Juliette?"

"I don't have an answer to that."

Dad leans back, runs his fingers through his hair, mulls over this unlikeliest of plot developments. "I'm sure you can understand why I wouldn't want you riding around in a car with the son of *that man*."

"Yes, Dad . . . but I'd understand more if we weren't just going right down the road."

"Most accidents occur five miles from home." He starts talking about this teenage girl he saw on the news who ran into a mailbox and killed herself. Unless she had a gun in the car, this outcome sounds highly unlikely, but I don't interrupt; my dad should get the words out of his system after spending all day, alone, in this dank room, trying to force them onto the written page.

When he runs out of cautionary tales, I say I'm going to walk instead, acting like it's a compromise that benefits him, too.

"Did you get the edits I e-mailed you earlier?"

Dad nods. "Thank you. You're the real writer in the family, you know." I walk over and kiss the top of his head, tell him that's not even close to true.

"This isn't like *a date* or anything, is it?" he asks as I'm walking out the door.

"It's nothing," I assure him. "Just wondering if he's someone I should hate."

I point to the computer like he could maybe use that line in his book, lock the front door behind me, and walk back toward Abram's car. He's right where I left him, eating.

He rolls down his driver's-side window. "Not bailing, are you?" he asks, already disappointed.

"Walking," I clarify, glancing back toward my house one last time.

Abram doesn't ask questions, just begins backing out as I

walk down toward the street. Instead of driving on ahead, he putters the car alongside me, talking through the window about nothing in particular. I smile. My lips are getting more exercise today than they have all year.

I wonder what my mother would've thought.

4

ABRAM

JULIETTE AND I are all alone in my house, the same model as her two-story down the road—the unwelcoming one with the blinds always drawn. Here's her right now: examining old photos and Christmas cards on the side of the fridge. Here's me: looking for an orange soda in said fridge. (The Paxil dulling my brain's receptors makes each wrong nutritional decision taste even better.) I reach past the bottled water I should be drinking and grab a can, popping the tab.

"You look alike," Juliette says matter-of-factly, pointing to a picture of my dad and me holding up an oversized tennis trophy. It was taken in South Carolina, last summer, the last tournament we played in together, the only one Mom didn't attend. Dad had me drive back to Virginia on my own. Only later did I find out Juliette's mom was meeting him there after I left.

I take a long drink of soda. "Yeah . . . sorry . . ."

"For?"

"Reminding you of him."

"Have you seen my face lately?" She doesn't turn around to show me how much she resembles her mother, just continues staring at the image, preoccupying herself with making sure her hair is still trapped in its bun. Setting my soda on the counter, I tell her I have to go to the bathroom and walk into the nearby half bath. I turn on the fan, flush the toilet, swallow my last Paxil to avoid getting a headache, and then come back a few seconds later, a bit worried she'll think I was taking a late-night dump.

I'm surprised to find Juliette holding my can of soda, risking the corresponding orange stains in the corners of her mouth.

"Thirsty," she says.

"Want one? I should've offered."

Juliette shakes her head, brings the can to her lips, and takes a sip that my grandma, she of the sugar-sensitive canker sores, would be proud of. As she slides the can back over my way, the note Mom left on the counter catches her eye. She starts reading it out loud.

Off to the casino with Aunt Jane, sweetie!
Make sure to let the dog out. Love you!!
Wish me luck! 777, Mom!

"Mom overdoes it on the exclamation points when she's excited about playing the slots," I explain.

Juliette's pupils contract into blank periods. The life comes back when she sees my golden retriever padding slowly into the kitchen with her eyes all squinty as if to say *You teenagers woke me up . . . and I'm glad you did. Come pet me!*

I appreciate Juliette leaning down and introducing herself to my dog at eye level, shaking her extended paw—good dog manners are important to me. The dog and I have been through some shitty times together.

"She likes you," I note.

Juliette looks up at me. "Doesn't she like everyone?"

"Not quite. She's been avoiding the neighbor's Labradoodle."

"Understandable," Juliette says to the dog, scratching her ears. "What's her name?"

" 'The dog.' "

I tell Juliette about how we tried several different tennis-related names—including Volley, Lettie, and Billie Jean King—but none of them stuck. I'll be the first to admit: boring story. But Juliette thinks it's a good example of how "naming anything is impossible," so maybe not.

"Want to sit down or something?" I ask.

She nods. We head toward the living room, sitting on opposite ends of the leather sectional.

"Do you still play tennis a lot?" she asks.

"Quit," I say, sprawling out across the cushions, my preferred state of being these days.

"Why?"

I'm honest with her about my lack of motivation, explaining that my dad had enough ambition for the both of us. After he was gone, I didn't have anyone to remind me there was a hungry group of runners-up just around the corner, waiting to steal our trophies, so we better get up a little earlier for practice tomorrow.

"Sounds like you made the right choice," Juliette says softly.

"Really?"

"No idea," she says. "I was trying to be supportive . . . ?"

We share a laugh—she gives me most of it, holding herself back. Why is she here, again? And why does she smell so good, even from over here, like . . . fancy laundry detergent and green tea extract? Meanwhile, the dog rolls over and allows Juliette access to her furry underbelly.

"You two really do seem like old friends," I say, failing to stifle my yawn.

"Maybe we met in a past life."

The idea of reincarnation sounds peculiar coming from her—she doesn't seem like the "back in the day, when I was a butterfly" type.

"Maybe you and I crossed paths in one of those lives, too," I propose, as casually as possible.

Juliette purses her lips like a girl who's been making this expression for centuries, thinks about it for a second, then surprises me by saying, albeit reluctantly, "Sure. But I think I might've been a whale."

"You'll never believe this, but me, too."

She's almost smiling as she rolls her eyes.

"Do you think we could've been friends?" I ask.

"Friend*ly*, yes," she allows. "Assuming our whale parents weren't associated back then."

I hold up my hand. "I'm almost positive they swam in separate pods."

She looks at me curiously, for a split second, before breaking eye contact.

We chat for a while longer until a warm blanket of mononucleosis falls across my body . . . disregard, it's an actual blanket, Juliette has brought over my mom's favorite throw and is covering me up. Damn you, Paxil.

"You don't have to go."

She starts to say something, stops.

"Were you this good-looking of a whale in our other life?" I ask her, one eye half open. I wouldn't bet money that I'm speaking English anymore. "What I mean is, would you have dated an ordinary whale like this?"

She sits down on the floor beside me, rests her head on the edge of the cushion. She looks like she's been fighting sleep for a while. I want to tell her to let it win, but turning it into an official competition probably wouldn't help.

"I'm guessing I was an emotionally unavailable whale back then, too," she says. "But I would've considered going on some kind of date with you, yes. Someplace where the water is warm."

"Now you're talking."

Content, I make my best approximation of a joyful whale noise. I may be beached right now, but I'm excited about my life for the first time in a long time. Even if it's a past life, in whale form.

Juliette says something else that I really want to process, but I'm drifting away, having some sort of hallucination now, seeing my dad in his casket—his cheekbones, broken in the accident, reconstructed with some sort of goopy mortician's wax. Mom's panicking. She can't remember checking a box saying YES to an open casket; thinks maybe she delegated the decision to someone else. I tell her I would've done the same thing. "People are probably thinking I'm a bad wife for letting him be seen like this," she whispers from our spot at the end of the mourning line. Those people aren't worth our time, but on this day, when Mom is being forced to pretend like everyone doesn't know about Dad and Sharon Flynn, the thought of their judgment is un-fucking-acceptable to me.

I walk over to the casket and politely ask a few respects-payers to stand back. Then I start trying to close the casket. I hear the various gasps and utters of "Oh my God," but I don't care; I'm problem-solving, protecting my mom. My dad, too, in a way. And yet the casket isn't really cooperating. I grab a different handle and pull down harder. The stupid . . . padded . . . lid . . . won't budge. No one looks interested in helping me out; most have backed away. The struggle continues until the funeral director shows up and Mom leads me away to regroup. She's not mad at me, very rarely is. We find a room to hide in and proceed to let it all hang out. We cry about Dad's face and how we'll never see the real him again. We get angry about his betrayal. We wish he would've been less one-thing-to-the-next, more open to enjoying himself with us, not just others outside our family. Then we start laughing at how the funeral director looked like he wanted to arrest me. Then we go back to crying because here we are, laughing at my dad's funeral, what's wrong with us? Mom says we're reminding her of "that one *Mary Tyler Moore* episode with the clown funeral" and I go "Oh, yeaaah" even though I have no idea what she's talking about. "If I tell you something about your dad, Abe . . . will you promise not to think any less of me?" I promise, and she whispers, "Sometimes I wonder if I ever really knew him." I tell her that makes complete sense to me, he was a hard guy to read. Then my mom's sister Jane barges in with a bottle of vodka and dares us to have an extra-stiff drink with her, which we do.

When I wake up, Juliette is gone. But it feels like she's here. There's also a chance I'm still sleeping.

5

Juliette

WHY AM I STILL HERE?

My throwing a blanket over Abram's admittedly decent body was the type of random act of kindness I'll look back on someday, a tear in my eye, and think, *Remember that one time I cared?* From the hallway, I watch as Abram flips around on his side so he's facing the back of the couch, blanket not quite covering him, his sweatpants drooping even further and revealing more than just a hint of butt-naked butt. It looks pretty much like what one would expect, if one were inclined to have such expectations: white, two cheeks, firm. And what about that bizarrely pleasant scent—a mix of shampoo, salt, and this morning's cologne—I picked up while sitting underneath him on a big pile of unswept dog hair? What about how I wouldn't mind smelling an encore?

I walk forward toward Abram, allowing myself one more

close-up of his cute face. It really does look like a younger version of his father's, and yet I'm still not hating his guts. What would it be like to lean down and press my lips against his? I bet it's warm there, near his breath. Might be nice not to be freezing for once in my life. Maybe kissing Abram would turn out to be the best thing I ever forced myself to do for no apparent reason.

Something's wrong with me.

I decide to give myself the grand tour of his house and reflect later, eventually ending up in the master bedroom. There's an iPad on the dresser; I touch the Home button and a paused game of Candy Crush appears. The bed Abram's father should've had enough self-control to sleep in more often is empty and unmade. Suzy Morgan has allowed a photo of their wedding day to remain on a stand beside the TV—bad choice. On the other side, a Zumba Blu-ray box sits unopened atop a good two years' worth of mint-condition *Women's Health* magazines. I'm not sure who's doing a less adequate job of taking care of themselves, this family or mine. Too close to call.

I wonder if Suzy read any of her husband's texting exchanges with my mom. That's exactly what I did while waiting around the hospital, went through my mother's personal things, starting with her cell phone. Wish I'd stopped reading after the first sext.

I force my eyes to swallow the hot tears welling up inside them—they don't taste nearly as good cold—and struggle with the urge to throw something at myself. That Yankee Candle on the nightstand, perhaps. I step into the walk-in closet before temptation strikes me down.

The hanging space and cubbyholes have been unevenly divided between husband and wife, Ian's tailored suits and shiny wing tips taking up the majority, too many of Suzy's garments getting the second-class Tupperware bin treatment. A year after her husband's death, Suzy's still afraid to claim what's rightfully hers. *Not acceptable.* I start removing blazer after blazer from the hanging rod and flinging them to the floor. Do the same with the wing tips. Then a bunch of shiny leather belts that look identical. I can smell Ian Morgan's woodsy cologne wafting up from the growing pile. If I were a garbage bag, where would I be?

Abram's still fast asleep in the living room when I grab a box of Heftys from underneath the kitchen sink. I go back to finish the job I probably shouldn't have started in the first place, before his mom gets home.

An hour later, I'm turning the key in my front door. I didn't come away from Abram's house empty-handed; took a roll of garbage bags (we're out) and my Doritos Locos Supreme, which I took a few bites of on the way home, but I'll deny that to the grave. I find my father passed out on the couch in his office. What is with everybody falling asleep today? I place a blanket over him, too, careful not to wake him.

I take my garbage bags to his bedroom, the place in the house he most avoids. I will myself into my parents' walk-in closet, which hasn't been touched since that night. I think about asking my father if it's okay that I do this, but I know his answer will be hidden underneath a mask that makes it impossible to tell if he really does care. I know that mask well, wear it every day, so I must be equally annoying to deal with.

My mother might have been selfish with her time, but she was very generous with her things. Shoes, lipsticks, perfumes—if it wasn't already on her person, I had carte blanche. *Oh, that smells so good on you, Juliette. Don't be a stinge—spray a little more. And definitely wear my Gucci belt with those jeans, yes?* My mother climbed the corporate ladder, made her own money, so there was really nothing wrong with her always having more of everything . . . except that everything was never enough.

Sharon Flynn lived in a world of scarcity, probably because her parents themselves died before she graduated high school; in response, she accumulated things, promotions, lovers. And who better to keep around as a backup than a man like my father with a large trust fund and zero desire to spend it? In other news, I need to quit googling "grief coping mechanisms."

I pick up a slinky black dress. The Chanel label I was once so enamored of seems so silly and pointless now. Just a word on a thing. Why are we keeping this? In case she needs a sexy cocktail frock in the afterlife? For me? I can't even bring myself to wear my favorite pair of her least-overpriced jeans. My dad certainly isn't going to jump up from the couch, grab an empty box and start organizing away, so I'm the default family member who has to place each item, once so essential to my mom's persona, into a stolen garbage bag. And rather than completely lose my mind to the sadness of what I'm doing, it's much easier to blame her for putting me in this position.

6

ABRAM

JUST HEARD MY MOM SCREAMING "Oh my God!" from another room. I throw off a blanket I can't accurately remember putting over myself and run to her bedroom. She's inside the closet, surrounded by a gang of stuffed garbage bags.

"Mom? You okay?"

She doesn't seem to be in any pain, although she's wearing a tight red mummy dress that looks like a challenge to move around in. Dad always liked her in red.

Mom turns to me, confusion in her eyes. "Did you do this, Abram?"

I look down again at the bags, then up at the empty hangers that once held my father's clothes. "Maybe?"

"Maybe, what?"

"Tonight's been kind of a blur."

"Have you been drinking?"

"Strictly Sunkist."

My mind flashes back to Juliette. Here. In my house.

Sipping from my can of soda. Staying awake through my boring stories. Watching me succumb to sleep. Bagging up my father's old clothes?

"Well, you've been meaning to go through this stuff anyway," I say.

Mom usually appreciates when I look on the bright side for her, but she's determined to crack the Case of the Walk-In Closet Organizer first.

"You didn't invite anyone over tonight, Abram?"

I hate lying to my mom, especially after what she experienced with Dad. Still, I'm not quite ready to tell the truth about this one.

"I may have had a visitor, yes . . . but it was nothing."

"Was it a girl?"

"It was a . . . Juliette Flynn," I answer, finally.

She gasps.

"I'm sorry, Mom. I saw her at CVS, and the hanging out just sort of happened on its own. Did you see I replaced your Big Red?"

She points to the gum in her open mouth, then says, "Of all the people you could have over past midnight, Abram, when I'm not home . . . you choose *Juliette Flynn*? Are you trying to traumatize the poor girl?"

"I thought you wanted me to check on her every once in a while."

"At school. Not in my bedroom closet!"

Technically, I wasn't awake when she was in here, but I don't think knowing that detail will help my mom come to terms. Eventually, I convince her this discussion would be better had in the kitchen while having ourselves a snack. She can't eat in the red mummy dress, though, and I step out so she can change.

I'm staring into the freezer when she walks in wearing her pajamas and fuzzy white slippers. She immediately locates the bag of pizza rolls I've been looking for and takes over the preparations.

"How is she doing?" Mom says quietly, staring at the microwave.

"She's . . . okay."

"Did she eat anything while she was here?" Mom nods back toward her bedroom. "She must've worked up quite an appetite."

"We had Taco Bell," I say, although I don't remember Juliette having any.

"Well, that's something, I guess." Mom places the plate of pizza rolls down at the bar and starts talking about stressful topics like eating better, cooking more often, and maybe doing some sort of cleanse together. Dad was always detoxifying something from his system, testing out the latest superfood, concocting the perfect tennis-recovery smoothie, making extra trips to the bathroom. Which meant Mom and I were joining him as guinea pigs in those efforts. Neither of us really minded.

"Hey, did you end up hitting any more jackpots?" I ask, changing the subject. I hold out my hand for an early inheritance.

Mom covers my palm with a napkin. "Aunt Jane convinced

me to play the five-dollar slots and . . . it didn't end well. But we had fun."

"The most important thing," I say, because she needs to hear it's okay to have fun again, and because maybe I do, too.

"Exactly," she says. "And I *did* get you a sweatshirt from the gift shop with my comp points."

I smile and act like the hoodie is a thousand-dollar bill when she brings it over and asks me to try it on. The sleeves are a little short for my overgrown arms, but otherwise it'll serve my purposelessness nicely.

"We're not done chatting about this Juliette situation, Abram."

I nod like a serious individual who faces tough topics head-on, hiding my nervous energy over the thought of Juliette and me evolving into a situation.

After Mom goes to bed, I wait about twenty minutes for her to give up sleeping and turn on her TV, then I ease my way through the basement door into the night. I cut across the neighbor's yard and follow the jogging path behind our row of houses straight up the hill to Juliette's. I'm trying not to make noise, but I've made a loud choice in footwear and my flip-flops are smacking. I take them off when I reach the edge of the Flynns' overgrown yard, the damp grass prickling against my feet. The blinds are all drawn except for one window on the lower level: the master bedroom, I gather, per the identical plans of our houses.

There's something sitting on the top of the dresser that

supplants my feeling of being creepy with one of hope. Her Doritos Locos Supreme. Just the wrapper remains, she's obliterated the rest, including the goopy innards that have a tendency to slide out of the unreliable tortilla shell. Knew she'd like it.

Then I see her—Juliette in the window, practically flying out of her parents' closet with a garbage bag over her shoulder. She flings it down onto the hardwood floor, swipes at the tears in her eyes, and turns back for more.

I want to help.

As if reading my mind, Juliette freezes, balls up her fists, and whirls around toward the window. She spots me right away, again doesn't allow herself the luxury of being surprised. I hold up my hand like I've come in peace, not to stalk her. She calmly lifts two of the bags, her twiggy arms refusing to give in to their weight, and then tilts her head down and to the right, where the hill the house sits on slopes toward the doors of the walk-out basement.

I meet her there. Neither of us speaks as I take the bags from her hands and haul them back to my house, my car, so I can deliver them to the Salvation Army whenever I wake up tomorrow afternoon. I lose official count of how many trips we make between houses. I'm too busy trying to grow on her, get to know her while not asking any questions, convince her there are no consequences to seeing me outside of school on a regular basis.

No idea if it's working.

7

Juliette

JOGGING.

A six-hour period of insomnia has passed since the premiere of my fake movie, *Prescription for Love*, starring me, in a role I was born to play, as "the crazy girl at CVS," and that other guy, whom I'm no longer allowed to think about starting now. One last thought: it was sweet how Anonymous took those heavy trash bags from my hands and didn't act like he was my knight-in-drooping-sweatpants for doing it.

Sprinting.

I'm home and stretching in record time. Brewing my father's morning coffee in what he refers to as "that fancy-schmancy machine your mom bought." (Doesn't help if I tell him, in an edgy tone, that *it's just a Keurig*.) I grab his mug and walk into his office. He's still asleep on the couch.

Looking down at his handsome face, the three distinct stress lines on his forehead, I make a wish to the fickle Writing Gods that he wrote a few paragraphs last night, even if they were horrid. I'll help him smooth over the clichés; I'm great with the delete key. He stirs, opens his eyes, and almost catches wind of my affectionate expression. Embarrassed, I quickly show him a picture of his mostly empty closet on my iPhone. Then another, as he sits up to process what I've accomplished on his behalf. He looks relieved. And also suspicious.

"You really hauled all those clothes out of here last night *without any help?*" he asks, eyebrows raised.

"I had pharmaceutical assistance," I say, handing him his coffee.

"I wish you wouldn't take that crap, Juliette. It makes you jittery, you can't sleep, and if anyone has ADHD around here, it's me."

"What? Sorry, I wasn't paying attention." I walk over and try to open the window, but it won't budge. "Why don't you join me today, Dad? There's this new thing everyone's breathing called 'fresh air.'"

I can't even see his mouth anymore, he's so against the idea. I'd have more luck reasoning with the three-hole punch on his desk. Then I see the wheels turning, his mind working like mine does when it's trying to escape the topic at hand.

"I'm serious about your Adderall," he says.

"I'm serious about your air quality," I say, from halfway down the hall.

I go back into the kitchen and make my coffee, staring at the picture of Mom's empty hangers. I'm not getting the hollow sense of closure that I guess I was going for. In fact, I feel more anxious than anything else, like I've made a mistake. No, that can't be it—maybe I just need a pill.

I unscrew the decoy Centrum bottle on the window ledge, taking out the CVS bottle I hid inside it last night. I pluck out an Adderall, break it in half, then decide to place both halves into my mouth, oops. I wash them down with a swig of my extra-bold, extra-black coffee. Once you go black, it's harder to go back to getting cracked-out on anything else.

I learned that from my mother, no stranger to CVS herself.

ABRAM

MOM INSISTED ON accompanying me to the Salvation Army this morning to drop off the clothes. She used the *Just want to spend time with my son* guilt trip on me, and it was hard to be, like, *No thanks, Mom—I'm all set*.

The problem with her being in my car as I pull into the parking lot is that I have about a million extra bags in the trunk from Juliette's house, and only a bad joke about those bags having babies overnight by way of explanation. I find a spot near the entrance and quickly get out of the car, Mom following suit. Reluctantly, I pop the trunk, and then box her out from trying to grab a bag and hoist her way to the chiropractor's office for the next six months.

"Abram?"

"You're not lifting any of these, Mom."

"Thanks, honey, but why are twenty more bags here than what we had last night?"

I start poking through some of them as if searching for

the answer. "They're all the same type of bag," I throw out there. Mom nods like that's really saying something, but I can tell she's still skeptical. She agrees to go inside and let them know we're here with a sizable donation.

I'm a few bags from getting away with not explaining myself when one of them starts to rip right in the entryway of the building, women's clothing items leaking out the bottom.

"Wait, are those mine?" Mom asks, rationally. She walks over and sorts through a few garments, picks up a black lingerie number with red cups, and holds it out in front of her. Not hers. She's frowning. This is tremendously awkward.

"I walked over to Juliette's house after you went to bed. Saw her hauling this stuff around, so . . . I helped. And I'm pretty sure that's not hers."

Mom drops the nightie (teddy?) when she realizes whose it was.

"I'm sorry, Mom." Not good enough, of course, but had to be said.

She shakes her head like it's not my fault, even though this reminder of it is.

"It's for a great cause, right?" she says.

I carry the rest of our donation to the counter as Mom speaks to the clerk. I overhear her saying that the women's clothing belongs to a "free-spirited cousin" of hers who moved to Oregon recently, the clerk nodding like, *What does that have to do with the 50¢ sticker I'm going to put on all of it, regardless?* Anyway, I love my mom and her free-spirited-cousin alibi.

Meanwhile, Juliette is probably leaving for her mysterious Saturday ritual right . . . about . . . now.

"I actually feel a little better about . . . everything," Mom says on the drive home.

"Me too, Mom."

She decided to keep four of Dad's bags.

8

Juliette

THIS CAB SMELLS to the point where I need to distract myself. Where did I leave off?

That's right, my mother and her Adderall habit. Well, she liked to refer to it as her "vitamin B12," more so back when I was a little girl who knew something was off about Mommy but couldn't put my finger on it. Back when we were as close as we were ever going to be. She'd get home twenty minutes before my bedtime every night and read me e-mails from her laptop in lieu of Dr. Seuss. She'd make a comment afterward, like, *Can you believe what Bob from legal is saying about this contract?* And I'd be all, *No, is he kidding us with that, Mommy? Anyway, I was wondering . . . could you sleep in my bed with me tonight?* Sometimes she would, and I'd fall asleep to the sound of her outraged typing. It was nice.

As I blossomed into a grouchy teenager, we drifted apart like all non-television mothers and daughters do. Then, a year or so before the accident, Mom developed a staring problem. I wish I'd reacted more calmly to being her target. Instead, I was more like, *What?* Not my best phase, but I was angry. Maybe even jealous because she'd begun allowing herself the luxury of giving up on the impossible: my father, his reclusiveness. When she started asking questions like *Do you talk to Abram Morgan much at school?* I knew. She'd found herself a replacement, a married man right down the road who'd appreciate her for who she truly wasn't. (It's easy to be an irresistably, sexy version of yourself for two-hour stretches, especially around someone who doesn't have to live with you.) From then on, the most I ever saw of her was at "breakfast," a meal neither of us ate. We'd sip our coffee, and every now and again she'd glance at me from over her mug, probably wondering if I was going to offload my suspicions to Dad. Turned out I didn't have to.

ABRAM

JULIETTE'S CAB SPEEDS down the road as I'm raking up the grass I should've mowed a week ago (that's what I get for ignoring the future like there's no tomorrow). Funny, she got a van this time. She never gets a van. I wave. She waves back but looks away while doing it. She's been crying. Have to stop myself from going over there and making everything worse. Hey, why is the van-cab pulling into her garage?

Juliette

MY DAD PAID two-hundred-plus dollars to get my mom's clothes back from the Salvation Army, not including the bribe I just gave the cab driver for helping me unload the bags into the garage. I don't anticipate him becoming aware of this, considering I went online and set all his bills to auto-pay a few months ago, after our electric got turned off.

9

Juliette

LATER THAT EVENING, my friend Heidi keeps calling me and getting side-buttoned. I don't even have the courtesy to silence the ringer and fake my unavailability—just send her straight off to voice mail. She deserves a best friend who doesn't hate Saturday nights and other people.

I decide to walk to CVS, maybe buy her a just-because-I-suck gift. She really likes those sporty headbands that keep the hair wisps from her eyes; the more vibrant the color, the better she plays tennis. I'm about to ask my father if he wants anything when I hear his fingers tapping the keyboard. I close my eyes and enjoy the sound of progress for a moment, then leave him be, quietly triple-locking the door behind me.

I slip out into the night in my all-black track jacket and yoga pants combo, your unfriendly neighborhood rape target. I walk down to my favorite jogging path, which happens to run toward the Morgan residence, a coincidence beyond my control. It's *muggy* out, the kind of late-September night that sweats on you, summer's last hurrah.

I take a slight right and weave along a narrower side path, drawing closer and closer to Abram's house. Someone's left on every single light in the place, blinds open, probably him. Didn't he say he lives in the basement? By choice? I creep down the slope of the lawn toward the sliding glass doors of the walk-out basement. I can see the right side of his face in the room adjacent to the living area. He's lying on what I guess is his bed, eating what looks to be pizza . . . on a bagel. Jesus. He's watching a nature show—hey, are those blue whales?—and looks oddly content to be doing what he's doing, which is nothing. He's also shirtless, for all my ladies out there who enjoy bare skin with tiny blond hairs on it.

Possessed by something cosmically dumb that I don't have the energy to question or make fun of, I hold out my fist and knock on the glass, right as it starts to rain. I watch Abram's brain process the sound, probably doesn't hear it very often unless he's got a late-night side-skank I'm unaware of, and he better not. He turns his head, sees me outside getting my bun wet—*Hi, I can't believe I'm here, either*—and I'm impressed by how fast and agile he is in jumping off the bed and bounding toward the door. His excitement kind of makes me want to laugh, or run in the opposite direction, or do an aerial cartwheel, which means I must be getting ready for my even-crazier time-of-the-month. Always something to look forward to.

He slides open the door and rushes me inside.

"Hey," he says, with more eye contact than I'm comfortable with.

"My laptop died," I say, looking around at nothing in particular. "Can I use yours?"

"Sure, yeah . . . it's over there being dusty," he replies nonchalantly, like I swing by for fake favors all the time. He has a knack for absorbing all the toxic energy I bring to a room.

I walk over to his dresser, pick up the computer, and there really is dust on it, he wasn't just saying that. I wipe off the top with a Taco Bell napkin I find on the floor and carry the laptop over to his bed. I sit down, sign in to my Dropbox account, pull up my dad's latest draft, and start typing over any future small talk. Abram must've expected me to take the laptop and leave, because he continues to stand off to the side until I give him a look like I'm probably not going to kill myself if he joins me. He flops back down on the bed and reunites with his bagel bite. He holds one out to me, I'm assuming as a joke, but I accept it just to keep him on his toes, biting into the crust. He nods like, *Good, aren't they?* He's going to be waiting awhile for my reply.

"There aren't any bugs down here, are there?" I ask Abram later, taking another bagel from his plate.

"Not that I've noticed."

There's a huge cobweb in the corner of the room. Intricately woven, as if the spider sensed she had all the time in the world. Am I going to let that go? I think I am. Because I feel comfortable existing here, in this space, with Abram and his whale show and his hidden tarantula. My mind is almost, but not quite, quiet.

"Is this whale show okay with you?"

"Fine, thanks."

"Cool," he says, and goes back to watching.

All conversations should be so brief.

Maybe we really did meet as whales in a past life.

10

ABRAM

I TOOK A PAGE from Juliette's book and pretended not to be surprised when she showed up at my sliding door last night. Between the dog and me? I thought she was either a super-dedicated UPS guy or a polite serial killer. She stayed until I fell asleep, which is another way of saying that once again I have no idea when she left. Her note on the top of my laptop said: *Thx for the Wi-Fi*. There looked to be the beginnings of an *X* or *O* toward the bottom, but I'm thinking that was an accidental pen mark. I put it in my wallet and saved it for my next rainy day.

The problem with good things happening out of nowhere with minimal effort on my part? Can't think of any, except maybe that I want the magic to happen over and over again afterward. So tonight I've been doing my best to re-create the miracle that was last night. Got the door unlocked, my snack at hand, a fresh whale documentary on TV, and my shirt in the off position.

Approximately two beluga segments later, I hear the door sliding open. I squeeze my fingers together in a silent fist pump because I knew she'd prefer letting herself in over the blah-blah formalities that go along with her knocking and me answering. She doesn't say anything when she walks into my room, just grabs my laptop from the same spot on the dresser, sits down on the bed, and opens it. Takes everything I have not to point out what I remembered to do for her.

"Thanks for charging it," she says, looking at me with a newfound something-I've-never-seen-before in her eyes. Seems too presumptuous to call it admiration. Appreciation, maybe.

I give her a lazy, it-was-nothing smile and proceed to fill my facehole with popcorn, letting her get settled for a minute before holding out the bag. She reaches her elegant hand inside and brings a few kernels to her lips. Then she does it again. I like this documentary, starring her in captivity, better.

Even if she's not into me, per se, we're definitely developing a connection per my snacks.

Juliette

HE SURE DOES fall asleep a lot. Must be the Paxil. He takes his pill and a half hour later it's like he's roofied himself. Now I'm sitting here, observing him like a science project, wanting more popcorn. I scrape the last kernel from our second bag and give Orville Redenbacher a look like I'm going to punch his face off, with all my rings on, for not putting more inside.

Then I wonder whose idea it was to make *that* face the face of the brand. His good friend, Colonel Sanders? Then I google "Orville R." and learn he died of a heart attack/jacuzzi drowning. I didn't need to know that, Wikipedia!

I should leave Abram a nicer note tonight. Something less robotic than *Thx for the Wi-Fi* with half an *X* at the bottom, which I'm hoping he mistook for an errant pen mark. Still trying to figure out why I started writing that kiss in the first place. Must've seen it in a terrible movie once—*Prescription for Love?*

Having issues focusing, obviously. Worried that I can't stop worrying about Abram's lack of tennis motivation, his excessive sleeping and eating and whale-show watching, his growing dependency on my unreliable presence, and, most of all, his Paxil prescription. All of this is a sign, right? A big red STOP sign with a *Seriously, girl, you've gone way too far* subhead. And yet my eyebrows continue furrowing. I'll have to pluck the movement out of them tomorrow. Meanwhile, let's check out these comments I just found on a sketchy online drug forum re: Paxil.

PaxilSkeptic: Worked okay at first, but then I gained forty pounds and became even more depressed!

BradG77: Ruined my life for the three years I took it, then experienced horrible zings and zaps, like I was being electrocuted, when I tried to get off of it.

JFWhatever: Why does anyone take this **** of their own free will?! Here's my prescription: Get some Adderall and go exercise!

Okay, that last person was me, just typed it in, couldn't help myself. In summary, Abram needs to get off of this FDA-approved brain poison—slowly, to prevent spontaneous electrocution—and I guess I'm the only halfway-invested bystander around with the organizational skills to help him do it.

I open up an Excel spreadsheet and name the file "Abram's De-Paxilization." I'm confident it's going to be the first decent plan he's had in a while. When I'm done, I leave him a note straight from my heart murmur:

> *Hi. We need to talk (without the TV on). I'll be back tomorrow night. Probably. And you were right—the popcorn was "extra tasty" tonight. I should have let you make a third bag.*

11

ABRAM

"WHAT ABOUT ADDING a 'Juliette' tab next to mine?" I suggest on night seven of her using my bed as a Wi-Fi hot spot, the second consecutive weekend we've hung out. I point to the "Abram's De-Paxilization" spreadsheet as she ignores my legit idea and reiterates the exact dosage I'm supposed to be taking each day to safely taper off the Paxil in under a month. When she's finished, I thank her for the detail-oriented plan.

"Why do you look like you're not going to follow it?" she asks.

"Isn't this the same face I've been making all night?"

Her eyes widen like, *Yes, Abram, that's why I'm not convinced.*

"Sorry, Juliette, I'm ready to stop taking this stuff. . . . I was just thinking it'd be more fun if I had someone to stop with me?"

"I can't be that person," she says.

"You *can* be that person. You just refuse to realize it yet."

"True. Plus, my withdrawals would be five hundred percent worse than yours." And with that figure in mind, she turns back to the computer and starts stabbing the keyboard, filling the "Abram" tab with even more clear-cut directions. I like to give her intermittent breaks from my presence, and now seems like an opportune time. So I mention something about making popcorn, her only known snack-food weakness, and sure enough she un-tenses her neck and tells me twice to remember the napkins.

I'm surprised to find my mom upstairs in the kitchen; Aunt Jane was supposed to pick her up for the casino a half hour ago.

"She's running late," Mom says, as I rip open the popcorn package and plop it inside the microwave.

"Aunt Jane's never late," I say, setting the timer and pressing Start.

"She was trying to make it past the Rainbow Runway on Candy Crush," Mom says, glancing longingly at the iPad by her purse.

"Are you out of lives?"

Mom nods, goes over to the cupboard on the far side of the kitchen, and pulls out the Crock-Pot. She's not slow-cooking a roast, just getting one of the money envelopes she keeps inside there, I'm guessing the one labeled CASINO FUND. Mom has a fund for everything. NEW CAR fund. NEW PATIO FURNITURE fund. ABRAM NEEDS $$$ fund. I put that one in there as a joke.

"Is there anything you want to tell me before I go?" she asks.

"Good luck?"

She knows. Moms *always* know, according to her. Not sure where the dads are when they're getting the eyes surgically implanted into the backs of their heads, but I bet my dad was familiar with the tennis courts in the area. Speaking of Dad, she's wearing red again, even though I overheard Aunt Jane, a loud phone talker, specifically forbidding it.

"Oh, and your hair looks good," I add.

"Really?" Mom touches her highlights, her face going through about fifteen different hair emotions. "I'm thinking of going a little darker next time."

She's always thinking of going a little darker, or getting bangs, but she doesn't really want to do either.

"Do you think your secret guest downstairs would like it?"

I give her what I hope is my most charming smile, but she's not having any of it.

"Would you do me the favor of at least sending me a text when you're planning on entertaining?"

I nod, even though I have no way of planning for that. I'm on Juliette's schedule. The spreadsheet she's modifying right now makes it official.

"And I want to meet her. Soon. Before it gets serious."

"Mom," I say, like she cannot be serious.

"I could just pop my head in and introduce myself right now, if that's easier for everyone." She walks toward the hallway, like she's heading for the basement. She can't fully commit to it. We both laugh, and then I'm saved by the car horn—Aunt Jane just pulled into our driveway.

"Gotta go," Mom says, kissing me on the cheek. "But I was being Strict Mom just then, you know that, right?"

"Yes. Obedient Son will get something on the books, ASAP."

When I walk back downstairs, I fully expect Juliette to tell me to get that *off the books.* But she's not there. Ran away, forgetting to take me with her. She took my dog, though.

Juliette

AS WE WALK ALONG the jogging path, I apologize to the dog for spacing out and thinking back, once again, to a few months before my mom died. I was in the kitchen stressing over my taking the ACT later that morning. Standing at her usual spot by the Keurig, a wry smile on her lips, Mom said casually, "Why don't you try one of my 'B12s' today?" She seemed genuine, like she wanted to help, not weaken my suspicions of her adultery with a bribe. I was putting just enough unnecessary pressure on myself to nod my head in agreement. "I'll make more coffee," she said, sliding a peach-colored Adderall across the countertop. I took it. Then I cleaned the kitchen, went to school, and made the ACT feel stupid about itself. The next morning Mom gave me an extra bottle she happened to have lying around in the cabinet where she hid her stash, and we laughed at the f'ed-upness of it all. Truthfully, I was relieved to be on the same page of crazy as her for the first time in a while.

The dog's tail starts to wag, responding to the familiar sound of flip-flops.

"I can't meet your mom," I say, when Abram catches up to us.

"Why not?"

Because he knows me too well already, for starters, having skipped over being surprised that I was eavesdropping.

"Because I don't feel comfortable introducing her to a crack-head," I say instead. "It's bad enough she had to share a husband with one."

I explain how Adderall and I came to be such an insepara-ble pair, introduced by my mother. Abram listens, waits a little longer than when it's his turn to talk, just in case I'm not fin-ished, then says encouraging things that discourage me from letting my habit define my entire identity. He's so *frustrating* sometimes.

"Do I really look like mother-meeting material to you?"

"More so than anyone I've ever met, yeah."

"Well, looks can be deceiving," I say. "I lie to you about food all the time."

"That's okay, I know how you really feel about the Doritos Locos Supreme."

I ask him to please not talk that way in front of the dog.

"By the way," he says, as we approach the basement, "if you're not mother-meeting material, then what kind of ma-terial are you?"

"The black kind. That doesn't go with anything else but black."

He laughs, asks, "And me?"

I'm about to say something off-putting like *Polyester!* but then I glance over at him trying so hard to keep up with me, still managing to be interested in this metaphor that I blame myself for starting.

I sigh. "You're linen."

Warm, unpretentious, counter-intuitively better with each wash.

"Linen," he repeats to himself. "Nice. Linen comes in black, too."

ABRAM

JULIETTE AND THE DOG continue walking slightly ahead of me until the dog sits down in the middle of the path, her way of saying she's over it. Juliette loves the dog's honesty, and their bond deepens, which I'm happy about. We turn back around toward my place, which I'm ignorantly starting to consider ours already. Ignorance is bliss trying to pretend nothing will ever change. That saying doesn't sound like me—probably borrowed it from someone. Juliette would tell me to give it back.

"We can do breakfast with Mom, less pressure," I say, as we reach the patio area. "You don't have to answer yet. Just think about it."

"Count me in as a firm maybe."

She frowns, slides the door open, and walks inside.

A short while later, she looks over at me and says, "Don't let her go darker."

"Huh?"

"Your mom's hair," she says patiently. "Darker is a mistake."

"I agree."

"Good," she says. "If we ever *do* meet, I don't want to feel sorry for her hair the whole time. I'll feel bad enough because of my mom."

I assure her everyone's hair will be in proper order except mine.

12

Juliette

HELP. FOR THE PAST few weeks I've been having trouble getting rid of something at school. It's standing next to my locker right now, actually, not falling for my disinterested-face tactic.

"I feel like skipping eighth period today," Abram says, even though he did that last Friday. It's the Paxil talking—still two more weeks of tapering to go before his last pill. He puts his hands in his pockets and rocks back and forth on his flip-flops, nodding in the opposite direction from class like I'm more than welcome to join in on the lazy.

"You could probably use the attendance points," I point out. Then we both start laughing for different reasons: me, because I just sounded like some sort of girlfriend he should break up with immediately; Abram, no idea—because he thinks laughing with others is fun?

I slam my locker harder than I typically slam it, once again trying to snap myself out of this companionship phase I'm going through. Abram doesn't flinch or say anything stupid, like, *Easy there, slugger.* He knows by now that, whenever possible, I prefer to slam doors. All the more disappointing that the one to his basement slides.

"I'll go to class if you hold my hand there," he bargains, once again forgetting to include what's in it for me. He just places his fingers between mine in his easygoing manner that's hard to object to, and the least-developed part of my brain—the prehistoric, reptilian lump of useless near the stem—signals that letting his warm-blooded palm incubate my cold one is smart, not dangerous.

As we walk down the senior hallway together, awkwardly entwined, another weird thing happens: A few of our peers smile at me like I'm *not* a loose cannon to steer clear of. This feels like a mistake on their part, in addition to mine.

"Do you think that Asian girl over there is pretty?" I ask Abram, testing him, wondering if I'm really his type, or if I'm just his type until that rare breed of slutty Asian drops into his lap.

"Only when she lets me cheat off of her," he answers, and I feel my grip tighten around his hand. I like the way he says the wrong thing sometimes. Also, the way he carries himself: his broad shoulders back, his stride long, easy, confident. Confident about what, I'm still not sure. Couldn't be his *Honey Badger Don't Care* T-shirt, practically a bare midriff because his long arms are causing it to ride up on his chest. Nor that overgrown organism of blond waves around his head. Or the perversely cute little paunch where his six-pack used to be that I'll miss when it's gone, because it's already shrinking. Or the butt I previously over-described a few weeks ago, barely hidden underneath the perma-droop of his sweatpants. . . .

"Has anyone ever told you that you think too much?" Abram asks.

It must be time for my pill. I pull a tiny fourth from my jeans pocket.

"Didn't you just take one?"

Yes, but that was a long time ago—several minutes, at least. He looks worried.

"Here," I say, casually transferring the pill from my hand to his. "To help you get through class."

He swallows it without a word, tells me he wants to know what it feels like to take what I'm taking. It's the nicest, most disturbing thing anyone has ever said to me. We walk into class together. Abram pumps his fist that our English teacher, Mr. Pewsey, hasn't come back from his cig break yet. I spot a familiar pink North Face jacket and a pair of long, tanned legs in the back row, where my friend Heidi likes to sit and not pay attention. Is there a nice way I can tell her to *stop wearing Crocs?* Never mind, I'm not ready.

I head in her direction, Abram ambling slowly behind. I find her leaning over and flirting with a lacrosse player I don't approve of. Heidi is perfect just the way she is, except for the Crocs and two more things: 1) Trust issues (she trusts way too many people), and 2) Bad taste in guys. She's the girl who'd smile and wave when the white van rolled up and the scraggly-haired guy inside who smelled like public-restroom soap offered her a dollar if she'd accompany him to his cabin in the woods. *Sure! Mind if my friend Juliette comes, too?* she'd reply, as I tackled her away from his extended hand.

I sit down in the desk beside hers and make myself uncomfortable. Abram sits directly behind me.

Heidi turns around, grabs my arm, and says, "We need to talk before Mr. Pussy gets back."

The nickname is still funny every time she says it.

"Did you remember my tennis-themed Halloween party this weekend?" she asks, seemingly unaware that she's double-booked the theme.

"Yes," I lie to her smiling, adorably freckled face that looks like it escaped from a Wendy's hamburger wrapper. "Not really, no. Where is it again?"

"My house," she says. "Well, my dad's house. Should I feel bad for hosting it while he's out of town?"

"Not when he still owes you for a lifetime of disappointment."

That came out exactly right, but wrong. Heidi looks less excited about the world now.

"Sorry, Heid." I sigh. "What can I bring to the party, besides a better attitude?"

"Hard liquor, if you have it," she says, "and a date." With a deliberately creepy smile, she nods in Abram's direction. I pretend not to know what she's talking about. "Yeah, okay," Heidi says, letting me play it my way. "Let's shop online for costumes tonight."

"Yay."

Shopping online with Heidi means her hovering over my laptop, talking about "getting deals," not letting me buy anything cute, and then forcing me to select something from this offbeat clothing store where almost all the inventory is colorful and sporty: her closet. Looks like I'm going as Maria Sharapova, which is fine, since I'm already wearing the bitchy-face part of the costume, 24/7.

I look back to check on Abram, see if he's having an allergic reaction to the pill I gave him, and maybe watch him do a little homework for the first time. He's picking a scab on his arm.

I send him a text that says *Stop it!* and he responds with a winky face. I almost reply that he's only allowed to text me winky faces when I can relate to the joke, but I have enough dumb rules to keep track of as is. Instead, I send him my specialty: a mixed message.

> Come to Heidi's party with me on Saturday?*
> *Please assume I still want to go when I try to cancel. ;/

13

ABRAM

THINGS WERE GOING so well until Juliette avoided her locker for the rest of the week, instead choosing to lug around her entire textbook collection from room to room, walking faster whenever she pretended not to hear me calling out for her. I didn't get the hint, just went ahead and kept fooling myself, thinking she might show up in my basement and be like, *Hi, sorry—you're not making popcorn tonight?*

Trust me, I made the popcorn. Every night. She remained a no-show.

Now it's Saturday morning, and I'm guessing Juliette's status for Heidi's party is "canceled," but I've already taken a shower per her instructions to assume she secretly wants to go. I may have to settle for walking over to the window and watching her storm into a cab in exactly four minutes. Still remember the first Saturday I saw her do this, a few weeks after the accident. I could tell she was having to struggle to keep it together but was refusing to succumb, her eyes glassy and sleep-deprived, the skin underneath shadowy. I almost knocked on the window that day, but there was never going to be a smooth follow-up to taking such an action, let alone a right thing to say. Couldn't pantomime to her, for instance, how watching her getting on with life made me feel like things had a chance to be normal for me again someday, too. No doubt they've been better than normal these past few weeks, in turn making it harder to go back to standing here, my breath fogging the glass, a completely separate entity from her.

I have to see her. Even if it's not on her terms. Even if there's never going to be a right thing to say.

I'll need help, though, which is hopefully where my mom comes in. I find her in the kitchen, distributing a huge wad of cash into the envelopes arranged on the table. She's been on a lucky streak at the casino lately, and I need to borrow some of it for a few hours, along with her car.

"Morning, Mom."

"Someone's up and ready early." She looks at me and smiles. "Come here, let me smell your hair."

I dip my head so she can sniff the conditioner she bought me, determine if she made the right decision. While she's deciding, I pluck her car keys from her purse.

"Mind if I borrow?"

"Did my son run out of gas again?" She's not asking this as a way to point out a past error of mine—just making conversation.

"Nope, he just wants to wash his mom's car."

She raises her eyebrows. "He does?"

"He does. Automatically."

She nods like *that's* the son she knows, hands me a twenty for the Ultra Wash, and then another twenty just for being me. It kind of feels like blood money I don't deserve . . . but we're blood, and it's not as if I'm drawing a salary from somewhere, so I accept it, promising to vacuum the interior, too.

Juliette

DON'T GET ME WRONG, I can tolerate Abram more than I've ever been able to tolerate a guy in my age demographic. I'm ignoring his existence now because I care. And I can foresee the dead end that will come from letting our feelings fester on and on, as long as we both shall not kill ourselves.

He needs to find himself a people-pleaser—a natural-born pushover who will do weird things like wear a special dress when the occasion never calls for it, forget to complain about going to the amusement park or a baseball game, and agree with his point of view for the sake of getting along. Like that musically talented Asian girl he cheats off of . . . but not, because I recently decided to hate that girl.

What Abram doesn't need is a problem-maker, and he's looking at her. The back of my shoddily straightened hair, actually, through the windshield of his mom's *candy apple* Lexus.

What is he doing?

According to the side mirror of the cab, he's singing. Doesn't seem to care if any passing cars catch him getting into it, tapping the wheel as he strains his neck muscles for a high note.

He's going to hurt himself. He's so . . . quick to embrace the present moment for what it is, even if he doesn't understand why I'm complicating it. I briefly consider teaching him a lesson he'll probably forget, but that kind of effort is what got me into this tailgating party in the first place. Besides, I don't want to keep this other guy waiting—the cute one I'm on my way to visit right now.

I unsnap a hidden pocket of my purse to make sure I brought him a treat.

14

ABRAM

THIS DOESN'T SEEM like Juliette's kind of place, but she gets out of the cab and power-walks straight through the entrance like she owns it, so I'm gathering we're here. I park toward the back of the adjacent lot and wait to see if anything more characteristic of her happens, like maybe she emerges with her earphones in place and starts pounding the jogging path that circles the building, or she brings a random laptop to one of the picnic tables outside, laments the slowness of the Wi-Fi, and gets a jump start on the weekend homework I've already forgotten about. With her, the sky's the limit . . . among other limits.

Thirty minutes later and she walks out of the Loudoun County Humane Society with a lucky dog: a pure-bred Saint Bernard with a shiny black nose, a well-groomed coat, and a long tongue that he's using to go to town on Juliette's hand. She doesn't seem to be enjoying the licking, but she tolerates it.

In conclusion, every Saturday morning, for the last however many months I've been window-watching her, Juliette's been volunteering at the Humane Society? Come to think of it, I *have* noticed my very own dog chewing some higher-quality bones lately—assumed they'd been stolen from my neighbor's fickle Labradoodle.

Just now noticing the twin daggers shooting out from Juliette's eyes—looks like they've been there awhile. In case there's any confusion over who her target is, she points in my direction and then makes a throat-slitting gesture with the same index finger.

I step out of the car, still excited to see her.

Juliette

MY DAD'S PRETEND-ALLERGIC to all animals, so the shelter's where I go to get my embarrassing weekly dog fix. Sorry, cats—I just can't, okay? Dogs are preferable because they have nothing in common with me. I've yet to meet a cocker spaniel who's addicted to her heartworm medication, a golden retriever with too many emotional barriers to count on four paws, a Dalmatian with unresolvable mother issues. . . .

The attractive young man at the end of my leash is Bing; I named him after the search engine, not Crosby, the depressing "White Christmas" crooner. Bing is a three-year-old Saint Bernard, but to any potential adoption applicants who inquire about him today, he's practically a *puppy*, and possibly a purebred descendant of a recent Westminster Dog Show winner, depending on if I get my first-ever believable feeling re: someone's ability to provide a loving home.

"Hey," is all Abram has to say for himself as we approach him. Bing doesn't play hard to pet, would much rather sit down on Abram's foot, lick the taste off his hand, and fall unapologetically in love.

"Why are you here?" I ask, annoyed that he smells good, like some sort of ocean-breeze cologne and the rosemary-mint conditioner his mom bought him last week.

He could ask me the same question, but just shrugs. "Hadn't seen you in a while."

He leans down until he's eye level with the dog while I try to think of something discouraging to say to that. I can't do it, so I introduce the two of them.

"Abram, Bing. Bing, blah."

The formalities over, Bing immediately flops onto his back so Abram can scratch his chest properly.

"I can take a hint," Abram says, winking up at me and scratching away.

Bing lets out a skeptical sigh, so I don't have to. Cute. Not sure which one I'm talking about.

"We still partying together tonight?" Abram asks me, skipping over the part where I've been crazy for the past three days. I make the mistake of noticing the hope in his eyes, digesting it long enough to feel a nagging pinch of optimism myself. *I'm not someone to get your hopes up over,* I try to tell him with mine, but I'm much better with non-verbal death threats.

"Sure," I say, covering the dog's ears. "If Bing gets adopted."

"Deal."

Abram insists the three of us shake on it.

15

ABRAM

I ASK JULIETTE if Bing's dad really medaled in a bunch of dog shows, as we watch him ride away with his new owners. She shakes her head no, her lips curving up, up . . . and this time the smile sticks. Her capacity for happiness is a lot roomier than she gives herself credit for. I ask if I can give her a ride home, and she can't think of a reason why it's a bad idea, probably because it's a win-win.

A short car ride later, I'm dropping her off at the stop sign at the end of our road. She doesn't want to further distract her dad if he's staring out the window when he should be writing, and her reasoning sounds pretty logical to a slacker like me.

"Don't touch his papers," I warn her, and her eyes narrow as she wonders how I latched on to that little detail, or maybe why I've chosen this moment to remind her I remembered it.

She opens the door, steps out, then pokes her head back inside. "Pick me up at seven thirty?"

"I'll be there."

She starts shutting the door, then stops. "In a cab."

"I'll be *in* there."

"Ask for Asad or Farrukh," she says, "and I'm really shutting the door this time."

"No rush."

"Abram?"

"Yep?"

"Thank you for following my cab today."

"Anytime."

She shuts the door less forcefully than she usually does.

Juliette

HE JUST SENT a text asking what kind of costume he should wear to the party. Typing in my response: *Don't ever text me while driving again!* Send. Sometimes I wonder if I'm coming off as too flirtatious—such a fine line.

His next message informs me he's at the car wash down the road, and also that he's lol'ing. Abram has "lol/ha-ha" disease—rarely sends a message without one or the other—but unlike everyone else in America, he almost always laughs as he's keying in the chuckles. I tell him I'll pick up something extra special for him at CVS, which also gives me a reason not to disturb my dad. The threatening *You better have some new material written when I get home!* text I sent him a half hour ago might be working.

Want me to pick you up there in 20? asks Abram's text.

Yes, please.

16

ABRAM

FORGOT HOW MUCH EXCITEMENT I can get out of a good, clean game of beer pong; I should start a league or something. Juliette wouldn't join. She's standing off to the side of the table, looking out-of-my-league in her red tennis dress, her hair tightened back in a low ponytail. She seems uninterested in the pong proceedings as well as her other Halloween-themed surroundings. Her best friend and my formidable pong partner, Heidi, is helping me keep track of Juliette's whereabouts in between throws. It's a tough job, but somebody's gotta stop my girl from French exiting before I can finally kiss her.

Juliette

ABRAM HAS SUNK every single shot at Heidi's portable beer-pong table tonight. Apparently that's impressive, because I've been watching from the sidelines like some sort of *That's my man!* pong groupie. Maybe I should leave without saying good-bye to anyone? *Such* a good idea, but then Heidi will get her feelings hurt, and there are only so many times I can right my wrongs with a package of headbands. Let me just grab my purse. . . .

"Where ya going, Maria Sharapova?"

Since when is Heidi so observant? It's like she has eyes in the back of her head tonight. Ironic, since there's also a plastic knife extending from her spine, the centerpiece of her Monica Seles costume.

"Just looking for my Chapstick," I say, holding up a closed fist of air like I've found it.

Heidi yells out a supportive "C'mon!" to celebrate my find—ever the best friend to my worst. She arcs a ball into one of the cups across from her and then holds her hand in the air afterward to rub it in. I like her playing style; the boys at the table are turning in strangely sportsmanlike performances. Abram gives her a high five as their two opponents, Jeff and Aaron, former teammates of Abram's who are both showing a lot of thigh in their identical Bjorn Borg costumes, seem genuinely happy for her success.

Abram sinks another shot and then adjusts the Andre Agassi mullet I found for him at CVS, picks a wedgie from the tight jean shorts he borrowed from Heidi, and smiles at me. I text him a half-smiley and then ask Heidi if I can use her phone. Instinctively she hands me the rubber cell-phone flask at the edge of the table, watches as I unscrew the antenna and make a call that tastes like a *wrong number.*

"Pretty smooth, right?" Heidi says.

"Rough," I reply through the flames in my throat.

"The next call will be better," she promises, taking a swig herself.

Half an hour later I'm still here, and Abram's carefully filling up the cups for rematch number eight. Haven't seen him this into something that doesn't matter since the whole being-around-me thing started happening. Here comes Heidi to check on me again.

"Having fun yet?" she asks.

"Getting there."

I bob my head once to the music for emphasis.

"Abram is such a great guy."

"Neat, why don't you date him?"

"Because I like my men five-seven and below, you know that." Heidi nods downward toward the dwarf licking his chops in the corner. I groan and remind her that the guy is a) grotesque, and b) in a weird relationship with the oblivious girl beside him. She raises her eyebrows like maybe he's not as off-limits as he seems, mouthing the word *hot* for extra-unfortunate emphasis. At a loss, I tell Heidi she looks pretty tonight, over and over again in slightly different ways. "Like a tennis player," I add, and that's the one she's looking for, all she's ever wanted to hear from anyone in lieu of the basketball-player comparison she unfairly gets. "The braid suits you."

"You mean it?" she asks, flipping it around so I can see it again.

"I do."

I don't love the braid, but I like that it's making Heidi happy. She should be in a Paxil commercial, dancing like she is now, encouraging others to join in on the joy, which of course Abram can't resist (if you count putting your fists in the air, rolling them around, and relying on your increasingly handsome face as dancing).

Is it really necessary to never make the best of anything just because life dealt me a difficult mom and then yanked her away before I could figure out what to do with her?

ABRAM

JULIETTE: LOOKS LIKE SHE has the world's most beautiful headache. Lips: Slightly pursed, redder than when I last stared at them. Cause: Mysterious ruby liquid she has been drinking from Heidi's revolutionary cell-phone flask. Idea: Maybe if I kiss her, she . . . would not want me to finish that sentence.

Can anyone tell I am thinking these thoughts in my robot voice? I am doing a subtle robot dance right now. I am a bit on the drunker side of the spectrum. I do not use contractions. I love pong! My ass hurts from Heidi, quote, "giving it what it deserves." I am giving this party an A+.

Juliette

HEIDI KEEPS TURNING UP the music. It's never loud enough for her until the beats are pounding in my rib cage. Here she comes with Abram; they're requesting my presence on the dance floor again.

"Please go away."

They can't hear me, but that's the closest I've come to saying yes.

Heidi points to her heart like she loves this song. More than the last one? Thought that was her all-time favorite. She pulls me out to the designated dance rug in the center of the room. Without giving me much of an adjustment period, she bends over and rotates her booty around in a disturbing helicopter motion, then twerks me up against Abram. It's really happening, only wish I could lie to myself that it isn't. Heidi's yelling, "Get it, Juliette. Get iiiiiit!" just in case I'm thinking of declining. I put up with it until I feel Abram's hands on my waist, barely, he would never be pushy about that. He turns me around toward him, snaps his fingers a couple of times, yet doesn't look stupid. A familiar urge comes over me. This time it involves *him*.

"I want to go somewhere," I say.

"Okay, sure . . . do you remember where I lost my hoodie?"

"No, I mean outside of state lines . . . for multiple days."

"Like a vacation?" he asks.

"If that's what you want to call it."

He points to himself by way of asking if he's invited. Somehow he does it to the beat of the music, pulls it off without looking like he's nailing a boy-band audition. Where does he practice these moves? His sleep? They have to be instinctual.

I nod, tell him he's invited. He swallows hard, trying not to get too excited, which is another smooth move on his part. He points to the random map of the world Heidi's dad has framed in the corner of the room, and I put my hands up, shrug, and then halfheartedly raise the roof to the music's *thump,*

thump, thump. I'm certainly looking dumb, but he sees potential in what I'm doing, tries to mimic it, but not even he can save it. Meanwhile, still in search of her fairy-tale ending, Heidi has waltzed off to dance between the dwarf and his girlfriend, who seem much more interesting when she's around. In her own inappropriate way, Heidi's setting a good example for me. That, right there, is how not to give a shit, let alone two of them.

"My family has a house on the beach," Abram offers. "My mom and I haven't gone for a while, but my dad was there last—you know that already."

Yes, I know. My mother was with him; the details were all texted out on her phone.

Should I bring anything special for our "work conference" at the beach, Mr. Morgan?

Just your tennis racquet, Ian Morgan texted back. *And don't pack nearly as many clothes as last time.*

Hopefully he packed some better pillow talk.

Perfect, my tear ducts are twitching with a twin set of drunk-girl droplets. My buzz must be stronger than previously denied to Heidi. Is my blood Adderall content too high to be drinking? No, I don't want that to be it.

"You okay?" Abram asks.

Not even close. I feel dizzy, but I want to show him I have enough mental stability left in the tank to take this trip, stay in a house where our parents slept together, without making it all about them. So I nod. Crack a smile. No teeth, though. Toothiness makes everything weirder. Abram smiles back, also no teeth, taking his antisocial cues from me like they're normal, yet another positive sign he's the best possible person to strand myself on an island with.

"Let's go to the beach," I say.

He nods like the decision's less complicated than it really is. "When?"

"Whenever. Or ASAP. Whichever comes first."

"Sounds good." He takes my hand and twirls me around to celebrate. When he draws me closer, to his chest, I swear I can smell the ocean on his skin, sea-salty and crisp. Cologne or potato-chip residue? That is the question. Until he asks a better one.

"What do we tell our parents?"

I frown, tucking his wig behind his ears. "We tell them . . . at the last possible second."

17

ABRAM

I TOLD MY MOM about our road trip the morning after Heidi's party, so pretty much right away. Took me the next five days to convince her to hand over the keys to our beach house. As of last night, she still wasn't blown away by the idea of me driving six-plus hours to South Carolina, with the standoffish daughter of my father's mistress, to stay alone together all weekend in the same house where *they* stayed a few months before their deaths. When I put all her least-favorite parts about the plan together like that in a series, I can better see the place of "Are you kidding me, Abram? You want me to call the school and play hooky for you, too?" she's coming from. Albeit from Juliette's driveway, at seven thirty a.m. on a Thursday morning, watching as my travel-mate kicks her giant suitcase across the threshold of her front door.

We're really doing this—skipping school today and

tomorrow, driving back on Monday (a well-timed teachers in-service day). Before Juliette can change her mind, I step out of the car and roll her luggage toward my open trunk. "You look like Grace Kelly," I say, hoisting it inside next to my carry-on. She was searching through Grace Kelly images on my laptop the other night, and today she's wearing a gray scarf of similar color to the one in Ms. Kelly's bio picture.

Her thank-you is followed by a short period of silence and then a nose crinkle. "I thought you were asleep when I was googling her."

"Same here."

The good news is she's still climbing into the passenger seat.

Once I'm back in the car, my seat belt snapped in place, she turns to me with renewed tolerance.

"Grace Kelly could really use some Starbucks, if that's okay."

Her belated way of telling me she approved of the compliment, and it's better belated than never.

"Prince Kelly of Monaco could go for some caffeine, too," I reply, pointing to myself and putting the car in gear. Her eyes dance with mine for a too-brief second before she places a huge pair of sunglasses over them. She knows I know that's not his actual name, or his British accent, right? If not, oh well—got what I wanted out of it: a start to this road trip, maybe even a promising one, if I do say so in spite of myself.

Juliette

ABRAM LOOKS DORKY-CUTE with his hat on backward, his hair sticking out the sides and still damp from the shower. His overall scent is dryer-sheet fresh; wish I could say the same for his car, which smells like a dead french fry.

"Didn't have time to shave," he says, his long fingers rubbing the dusting of stubble on his chin.

"Hadn't noticed," I say, cracking my window.

Too harsh. Try again.

"You can pull it off, sort of."

"So you're saying you like it?" he ventures, glancing over at me as he puts the car in reverse.

Yes. But can I be honest about that?

"As long as it doesn't turn into a scruffy beard and a part-time job at the Apple store," I allow, removing an air freshener from my purse and tying it around the knob of my closed vent.

Who would've imagined there'd be a beachside sequel to *Prescription for Love*? Not I, says the pill-popping Grace Kelly wannabe who could've sworn she quit the industry a few weeks ago. Not my dad, after I mentioned the trip to him in passing, hollering out the details as I walked by his office. He wasn't amused, went so far as to threaten canceling his credit card that's been making itself at home in my purse the last three years. I was proud of him for standing up to me, via e-mail. Still feeling guilty about not replying, and for leaving him to his barely operational devices.

Are we there yet?

Close, we're just now crawling by Abram's house. He's checking on his mom one last time, anxiously clicking his tongue. Their yard looks good, like the people inside the house care; Abram mowed it last night, in the dark. Washed her car again, too.

"How's she doing?" I ask.

"She's . . . still getting used to the idea."

"Of hating me?"

I immediately hate myself for the question, and the guilt in my voice. It doesn't take a boy to realize this getaway of ours has "crazy girl" written all over it; it takes a mom concerned enough to pay attention. Jesus, I think she just sent him a text. I can't bear the thought of her standing there, helplessly texting through the window. So I don't. I take out my phone and start deleting productivity apps. I feel like a terribly productive person.

ABRAM

My mom's last words to me before I drove off into the sunrise didn't sound like her, so I suspect she borrowed them from my outspoken aunt Jane: "If you two *high school seniors* want to pretend you're all grown up now, then when you get back, we're going to sit down and have an awkward meal together with lots of forced conversation . . . like real adults do." The text she just sent as I was driving by the house was more her style: *Still worried but sorry for going all "Aunt Jane" on you. Have fun—that's the most important thing, right? I love you, be careful, text me when you get there!!!*

Juliette

"MY MOM DOESN'T HATE YOU," Abram insists, sliding his cell back into his pocket. "She just wants to meet you."

I look up from my phone. I promised him that, didn't I?

"Not ready yet," I tell him, looking back down. If only Suzy Morgan could be aware of my intention to never become pregnant with a baby alien, without me making good on that face-to-face . . . she'd probably still be a hater. But surely she knows her son wouldn't create something sexual out of thin air. Then again, he's pretty excited about this trip.

"Here," I say, handing Abram my Starbucks Gold Card as he rolls up to the glowing menu. He takes me to the best drive-thrus, often. Now he's looking around for his already-missing wallet, running his hand underneath his seat, emerging with a beautiful bouquet of crinkly straw papers. For me? The employee manning the loudspeaker manages to thank us for choosing Starbucks, even at this hour, and then asks for our order.

"Your usual?" Abram asks me.

I've developed this unfortunate habit of leaning over him and ordering for myself. Doing it again, trying to yell out as politely as possible, still sounding like a swashbuckling lady truck driver. Abram pulls up to the window, pays with my card, and hands me one of my two drinks, placing the other in the cup holder beside his; I put his straw in for him, finding our early-morning synchronization to be quite scary.

I hand him his wallet and ask him to pull up beside the bench in front of the store.

He looks over to make sure I'm serious. "The one with the dead homeless lady on it?"

"Yes, that's Claire . . . I think."

Last week she preferred Georgette.

18

ABRAM

JULIETTE HIDES MY WALLET AGAIN, this time where I can see it, before opening her window and shouting, "Claire!" The woman jumps up from the bench and walks over to the car, quicker than she looks. Juliette holds out one of her two ventis and says, "Morning," minus the good in front of it. Claire mutters an "Mm-hmm" in response, clearing the cobwebs from her eyes. Looks like she's got some on her clothes, too, but those are less of a concern. She takes the coffee from Juliette's hand and says, "You're so sweet to me, girly."

"You can do better," Juliette insists. She waits for Claire to take her first sip before asking if the coffee's strong enough. Claire waves her hand back and forth like a connoisseur not quite ready to commit. Juliette hands her ten dollars, explaining she'll be gone for a few days.

"Excuse me?" Claire asks, like a homeless mother figure caught off guard. "Where to?"

"The beach."

"With him?"

"What's wrong *with him*?" Juliette demands, which makes me smile.

Claire puts her hand over her eyebrows, trying to get a better criticism vantage point. I'd tip my cap in her direction, but it's on backward, so I just nod.

"Cute," Claire admits to Juliette. "Smiles a lot, though."

"Somebody has to," Juliette says. Claire forgets about me and begins talking about the ladies she plays bingo with at the church. Juliette's finger points forward, beneath where Claire can see, indicating I should drive away from the story.

"You help homeless dogs *and* people?" I can't resist bringing this up as I'm merging onto the highway slowly, but not too slowly, trying not to scare her as she tenses and tightens her seat belt.

"Claire's my last one." Then, looking more amused, she adds, "My dad thinks she's faking her homelessness."

"Really? Never thought of that."

"Good, that means you're not crazy."

"What do you think?"

"The worst," she says. "Easier to avoid surprises."

I raise my eyebrows and point to myself, like, *What about this surprise?* She scrunches up her nose, still looking for a way to explain away the whole me-and-her phenomenon. I don't think there's a scientific explanation.

"Was he—your dad—better with everything this morning?"

"No. But he silently handed me some emergency hurricane supplies on my way out." She removes several items from her enormous purse: a wind-up radio, water purification tablets, flashlights, a flame-retardant blanket, and a Nylon Paracord(?). "He even left the house to get it all," she says, a slight uptick of pride sneaking into her voice.

"That's awesome."

She waves away the awesomeness. "We all have our milestones, I guess."

I almost mention she's reached one herself, by suggesting this trip in the first place, agreeing to get to know me out-of-state and hundreds of miles from her comfort zone. Instead, I say, "Possum chunks," motioning to the dead animal on my side of the road. Juliette doesn't get grossed out by the gory randomness of my icebreaker, just raises an amused corner of her mouth and continues staring out the window.

"Deer carcass," she notes, a minute or two later.

"Where?"

"Up here on the—never mind, don't look." Grimacing, she uses her large purse to block off her section of the windshield from my view, but she's too late . . . what the hell?

"Was its head completely detached?" I ask her.

"Yes, but trying not to think about it."

"Sorry."

A few minutes later, she puts her game face back on and says, "Squirrel remnants, on your left."

"Good one."

With all due respect to the roadkill, there's a silver lining to be had here: Juliette's playing my new game without me having to beg or poorly explain the rules (*It's just like spotting a padiddle and calling it out before someone else, only with animal guts*). If she asks me, we're officially on vacation. She won't, though. That's more my type of question. I'll hold off till our feet touch the sand.

Juliette

ONLY FOUR HUNDRED miles to go. Whenever Abram makes a sharp turn, I hear the rattling of a pill or twenty against the plastic bottle stowed inside the front pocket of my purse. It gives me a sense of car-ride calm that I'm not proud of but otherwise couldn't achieve. Not without making a drunk dial from Heidi's cell-phone flask, which somehow found its way into my suitcase during her unannounced but ultimately enjoyable visit to my house last night. I regret not putting the flask, a leak waiting to happen, in a freezer bag. (Hopefully she gets a replacement when her contract renews.)

We've cruised by two police cars in the last five minutes, so I tell Abram about the flask, the second-most-responsible thing I can do after not bringing it in the first place. (*So where's the meth lab?* the highway patrolman will ask after he finishes his search through my things.) Abram's not fretting the legalities, if his jokey fist-pumping is any indication. I appreciate how he puts the same hand right back on the wheel before I start pressing my foot against the nonexistent passenger-side brake. There's nothing less masculine than a guy who acts like he has too much testosterone for two-handed steering.

"Let's stop at a gas station and get snacks soon," I suggest.

Keeping his eyes on the road, he reaches over and pats my

arm gently—I think he was looking for my hand (it's underneath my leg). As he's maneuvering the car around the exit ramp, I pat his arm back.

"Where are we?" I ask, handing Abram the bottle of coconut water I bought him, trying to keep him hydrated between caffeine spikes. It's his job to keep the snack crumbs from accumulating in the crevices of his shorts, but apparently he's trying to get fired.

"The interstate," he says, scratching the back of his neck and shooting me a reassuring smile. "We're on the right road, promise."

I turn on the GPS, then spend the next five minutes trying to change the lady's accent to British. I'm one of those people with too much time on her hands, letting the wind take me to unproductive places where I mess with the settings of electronics. Then I remember that's the whole point. The underarching theme of the trip, even. To sit still long enough to find a part of my personality I enjoy being around more, or become a completely different person who doesn't dissect her personality into parts.

"Wanna play the capital game?" Abram asks.

"Yes," I say, as quickly as I've ever agreed to anything. I used to play the same game with my dad—on our way to getting office supplies and Starbucks, not a big bowl of disgusting ice cream.

"Mont—"

"Helena," I answer, giving him a girlish fist-pump of my own. The maneuver is missing most of his humor when I do it, but he laughs anyway. I hide my embarrassment by getting more serious than the nothing we both have at stake warrants and saying, "Norway."

He bites his lip, probably thinking we were quizzing each other on U.S. capitals only, and this is why I'm not someone people should root for.

"Never mind, let's just do states," I say. "Virginia."

He shakes his head like everything's under control and says, "Oslo?"

I'd be as shocked as the Norwegians if I didn't already know Abram's been sandbagging his potential around me. Which is why I put his big pile of unopened mail in my bag last night, after he fell asleep. Maybe I *am* that thing. The girl-thing who's going to turn him into college material after all.

19

ABRAM

I DEFEATED JULIETTE in one out of the many capital games we played—thank you, Lithuania!—but we're not allowed to talk about it until she's had enough time to figure out what's gone wrong with the world.

Good thing we're almost to our destination, just crossed over the bridge and onto the island. Forgot how much friendlier people are down south—perfect example being the personable woman with the bright-red lipstick at the toll booth back there, who seems to be having one of her best days in years. I open the windows and slide back the sunroof, in case there's an element in the air we can get in on. (There's definitely some NaCl, Mr. Kerns, so does that make up for me skipping Chemistry today, tomorrow, and possibly Tuesday?)

"It's nice here," Juliette says. Then she coughs a couple of times and closes her eyes, enjoying the wind in her immovable bun. The relaxation lasts a minute or so before she's removing one of her two jackets and turning her heated seat down from High to Low . . . and then back up to Medium. Sitting up straighter, she cranes her neck around toward her open window, trying to see as much of the ocean as possible. Makes me feel like we've made the right irresponsible decision.

We stop at the Piggly Wiggly to pick up a few groceries, and I only oink three or four times while we're there. Juliette oinks once in the frozen-foods section, but softly enough to keep her dignity. Twenty minutes later, I'm creeping the car through the gates of our private neighborhood, holding up my permit to the Kindle-reading security guard, who grins and points to his device like he's got a real page-turner in his hands. I glance in the direction of the country club as I roll the car over a speed bump, past the tennis courts where my father and I used to hit for hours. Clay was his favorite surface to play on. And mine. I catch Juliette making a mental note of my interest in the courts, but then she turns away before I can take notes with her.

Our house is the last on the street. Looks a lot like the others—picturesque, manicured, surrounded by palm trees. On the front side, the sound of palm fronds rustling in the breeze is pretty much a constant. The back of the house sits up against the beach, protected from the tide by a sand dune. Juliette's staring at her arm, and for a second I wish we could ride around town for the next four days instead of going inside—that way, I could guarantee we wouldn't find some sort of immediate setback left behind by our parents. But suppose we did drive away from any potential difficulties inside . . . then what? We'd still be the same people regardless of our surroundings, and eventually our pasts would catch up and be like, *Hey, guys, remember how shitty we were?*

"C'mon," I say to Juliette, "let's go have some fun."

"Even if it kills us?"

"Nope." I turn off the car and jiggle my keys. "The alive-only kind."

Juliette

THE MORGANS' TWO-STORY beach house might be considered charming by someone with an easily charmed outlook on life. To me, it looks overwhelming. Also, keeping Ian Morgan's "travel lightly" text to my mother in mind, I definitely overpacked. The veins are popping on Abram's arm as he carries my suitcase toward the door.

"You should just roll it, yes?" My third time telling him this, but who's counting?

"Nope, not a problem," he says, adjusting his grip between breaths. He hoists my problem up the stairs of the wraparound deck and through the front door, which, in my reluctance to go anywhere near the house, I almost forget to hold open for him. He steps inside, and I'm right behind him, in spirit. I hear the suitcase rolling along the floor as I'm shutting myself out. Removing my phone from my purse, I try to think of something to text my dad, but nothing seems appropriate given that this whole situation is somewhat inappropriate. I decide on: *Here. Love you.* A few tense hair adjustments later, I get his comparably affectionate *Thanks—love you, too* response. Nice to know he's still the kind of parent who can be the bigger person.

"Ready for the grand tour?" Abram asks, walking back out a minute later.

"Don't forget to text your mom," I say, putting away my phone.

"Next thing on my list." He smiles because there isn't any such list as I look down at his long fingers, still outstretched in warm welcome. Not for the first time I notice how veiny and sinewy his hands are.

"What are you thinking about?" he asks.

"The ocean."

And strong hands. Back at his basement, between sea-creature documentaries, Abram will go outside but leave the screen door open in case I need anything, and I'll hear him clipping his nails for a solid twenty minutes, disturbing the locusts for a change. The effort obviously isn't lost on me, but who knows where the self-control hides when it's time to fill out college applications. Probably the same hole mine's crawling into right now.

Without warning, Abram does exactly what I wasn't prepared to admit to wanting all along. He reaches out and presses his cushiony palm against my bony counterpart, which is eager to escape its cold, low-blood-pressure prison and burrow into his skin as our fingers slide into place together.

"Promise not to run away?" he says.

"Never."

As in, *Never promising that.* Abram knows what I meant.

"I'll let you run beside me if I do," I add.

He squeezes my hand.

20

ABRAM

THOUGHT IT MIGHT help Juliette get settled if we went upstairs and unpacked immediately, without so much as stopping to turn on the TV. Bad call, the dread seems to be settling in as we stand just inside the entryway of the master bedroom, staring at the intimidating four-poster king. The floorboards creak every time one of us moves, and it wasn't just her paranoia expressing itself a second ago; I think it *is* colder in this room versus every other room in the house. The peppermint-scented cleaning products and the pale-blue linen duvet are subtracting a few more degrees, as is my dad's metallic-gray tennis racquet leaning against the closet door.

"Maybe we should sleep downstairs," she suggests, already leaning in that direction. "Where there aren't any ghosts."

"There's a ghost-free couch bed in the living room," I say.

"Sounds lovely."

We roll our suitcases back down the hallway, past the other available bedrooms, to the top of the stairs. Juliette tells me just to push hers down and let the suitcase land where it may, but that sounds like a red herring option whereby the girl is temporarily convincing herself she won't blame the boy for whatever happens. I grab the handle and lift, taking a break every few steps because she keeps recommending it. One of these days, she'll let me perform a favor for her without calculating what she owes me, which is always going to be nothing. Except maybe a kiss, if our relationship ever reaches the level—pinnacle?—where favors can be repaid sexually (in a respectful manner).

Once downstairs, we pull out the couch bed and cover the mattress with as many sheets and pillows as we can find outside of the master bedroom, topping it with her dad's flame-retardant blanket. She's already predicting how cold she's going to be tonight. My theory on that is she'd be less freezing if she'd stop mentioning it out loud, like self-fulfilling body temperature. It's not very well thought-out, but it still feels like I'm onto something.

"You sure you're okay with staying down here?" she asks, as if I'd nitpick the conditions in which I get to sleep with her completely awake beside me.

"We can do whatever we want," I remind her, smiling. "There's no right or wrong on vacation."

She frowns, looks like she's thinking this over until it sounds more wrong in her brain. Then she says, "You're right."

"Not necessarily."

She arches an eyebrow, perhaps impressed I didn't fall for her trick. Perhaps not, but I leave it at that and turn on the gas fireplace, which makes her happy. By the time we have everything situated in our ad hoc bedroom, the sun is setting. Juliette asks if I'm hungry, and I'm like, "Hell, yeah!" The immediacy of my enthusiasm startles her.

We head into the kitchen and she has a seat at the bar as I gather the makings of several multi-ingredient sandwiches. She answers my "How many?" question with a "Zero."

"Already ate," she insists.

I stare inside the fridge for a minute, trying to remember that occurring recently.

"Food?" I ask, shutting the door.

"Pill," she says, as a load of fresh cubes crashes into the ice maker.

Her choosing Adderall over a sandwich may not be wrong by my lax vacation standards, but it still feels like a sore subject that needs to be addressed while we're here.

"Speaking of pills, guess what tonight is?" she asks.

"Tonight I'm officially Paxil-free, thanks to you."

"A monkey could have made that spreadsheet," she demurs.

"No way. But what about a Piggly Wiggly?"

She groans, swiveling back and forth in her bar stool. "So . . . are you feeling depressed right now?"

"Yes." I reach into a nearby cabinet and set an empty plate down in front of her. "But only because you won't have a sandwich with me."

21

Juliette

AND THIS IS WHY I rarely bring up the truth about myself—Abram gets all low-key worried about a lost cause. I'm blowing air into my cheeks to make my face appear more well-fed, and it might be my least effective ruse yet; for sure the least attractive. Right now he could easily point out all the reasons I shouldn't be taking Adderall, including death of appetite, so why isn't he? He's opting to say nothing at all, which is . . . making me hungrier?

"What about half a sandwich?" I hear myself say.

Abram flashes me a relieved smile, wags the butter knife in my direction like I won't regret this, then begins the multi-ingredient congealment process. Every once in a while, he'll look toward the door like he's expecting his dad to walk in at any moment, and my heart attacks me. In defense, I picture my mother walking in on the arm of Ian Morgan, acting like the four of us are on a perfectly deranged *couples retreat* together, and then heading straight for the wine bottles that line the top of the cabinets as I slip out the back door. She'd have a much easier time lighting up the room without me, I'm sure.

"You ate your whole half," Abram points out, smiling. I look down at my plate. Empty. Hunger blackout.

"Want to test out the hot tub in a few?" he asks, pointing toward the back of the house, as if the convenience of the location will make it harder to resist.

"Only if we can get tested for staph infections afterward."

"There's an urgent-care down the road," he says, laughing.

I'm serious, just ask Heidi about her leg wound that bubbled open for two months after she took a dip in a hot tub—she's fascinated by the experience now, having had plenty of time to make peace with the disgustingness of it. (I'm going to need a few more years.) I wish Abram had asked me a question I could've said yes to, even though he seems fine with yet another no.

"How do you do that?" I ask.

He points to his chewing mouth, like, *Eat an abundance of sandwiches?*

I shake my head. "Accept everything, all the time, even when there's no good reason for it."

He swallows. "Why fight it?"

"Because otherwise it will never change?"

"It's more likely to change if I don't force it," he says, an understated confidence to his tone. "I could teach you how to go with the flow sometime, if you want."

"You already have been," I say, without sarcasm. "Just keep doing what you're not realizing you're doing."

"Will do," he promises, as I wipe a crumb from the corner of his lip. "Unwittingly, of course."

My hand freezes by his face for a second.

I stand up and throw away our paper plates—before he can see the goose bumps on my arms—and watch from the corner of my eye as he stretches, pats his stomach, and then yawns, not all that concerned about whatever's not going to happen next.

"Okay," I say, "let's go hot-tubbing."

That must be the new Juliette talking; she's a gung-ho hobag who's totally down for mostly naked and highly unsanitary experiences. Meanwhile, the old me is like, *Girl, good luck with her. I'll just be over here thinking about where to hide your pills from the ghosts.*

As Abram and I head toward the living room to change, I look back at the kitchen one last time, mentally apologizing to my mother for making up a back-from-the-grave scenario in which I wasn't happy to see her. Maybe my negativity patterns will stop repeating themselves in the hot tub tonight, or at the beach tomorrow, or neither because I'll be wearing a swimsuit.

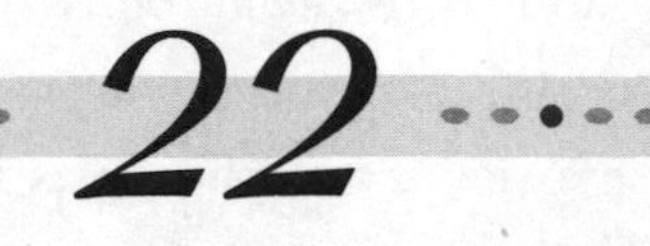

22

ABRAM

I've grown accustomed to my mom asking if I remembered to pack this or that until she just ends up doing it for me, so it's still not her fault I forgot my swim trunks, but that's why they're back home in a pile somewhere. This oversight reminds me to send her a text saying we got here safely and the house is okay, so all isn't lost. Mom texts back an immediate thank-you, with multiple exclamations, then sends a picture of herself and Aunt Jane smiling next to a slot machine, three diamond symbols glittering up the screen. Seconds later, Aunt Jane texts:

> You owe me a souvenir for keeping her entertained, Mr. Romance. (And, yes, I realize we would've gone to the casino anyway.)

She thinks of everything, Aunt Jane.

I put on a pair of swimsuit-looking gym shorts while waiting for Juliette to finish changing in the bathroom. She's been in there awhile, probably being overly critical of her flawless appearance. "Hey, you need more toilet paper?" I call out, trying to stop the critique by implying she's taking an evening poo.

She flings open the door a second later, wearing a custom death-look that makes it harder to stare at her in that red bikini, but I still find a way.

"I wasn't . . . you know."

"Of course," I say, like a distinguished gentleman. I hide my snicker behind the towel I'm offering to her. She throws it back at me, grabs her huge purse, and walks toward the door. Perhaps a reluctant dip in the hot tub will help her relax.

As we step outside, the whole backyard scene—the sandy deck underneath our feet, the sound of the ocean crashing predictably against the shore—does seem less to her hating. There's another shift in mood as we close in on the hot tub and remove the cover, and the motor starts whirring like it's been waiting for company to come. My right foot is almost touching the swirling, foamy water when she holds out her palm in warning.

"Orville Redenbacher died in a hot tub," she pronounces.

"The popcorn guy?"

She nods and waves me away from the danger impatiently, until I step down.

"Did he drown in it?" I ask, as we place the cover back on.

"After his massive heart attack, probably . . . Can we go to the beach?" She grabs my towel and hands it to me. "I need to make an emergency phone call, and so do you."

"Yes," I say. "Several of them."

As we step onto the sandy boardwalk, she tells me about poor Orville, and then another cautionary tale involving Heidi and a hot-tub-related staph infection that makes my foot tingle like it's been saved from amputation. The wind picks up as we near the water's edge. We stop just short of the lapping waves, sit down in the sand as she tells me she's sick of the sound of her own voice and removes Heidi's cell phone from her folded towel. We take turns making liquid 9-1-1 calls from the antenna spout, sending fake texts from the rubber keyboard in the interim, enjoying each other's company minus any disruptions from nonfictional technology.

"You sure it's okay for you to be drinking on Adderall?"

"Yes, according to my doctor." Her poker face is less convincing under the influence, so she turns her head from me and takes her next swig in private.

"Maybe I should give him a quick buzz," I say.

Juliette hands the flask back to me so I can knock myself out. As I'm fake-dialing, she says, "Want to go skinny-dipping?"

I forget about everything and start glancing around, spot a few flashlight beams in the distance—people hunting for crabs, not the police coming to arrest us, as Juliette suggests. They're a good mile or so away. For all impractical purposes, we're alone.

I look back at her. "I shouldn't take that proposition seriously, right?"

"What if I'm serious?"

"Then . . . I don't know . . . let's be serious about it?"

She stands up as if she'd like to see someone stop her. I am not that guy. Right now, I'm the guy who's starting to take off his shirt.

23

Juliette

THIS IDEA IS LOSING the little appeal it had now that I'm standing upright, the wind gusting through my skin. I look down, rake the sand with the bottoms of my toes, having just remembered something truly awful about myself . . . my body! It's *not* on-point—just pointy, best viewed in the pitch darkness, or in an asexual one-piece, definitely not in all its bikini-free glory. Abram, possessing no such hang-ups, is already stripping off his salmon-colored T-shirt, the one with the holes and the dangling strings that I've been meaning to misplace for him. He gives me an impish look, like he's about to get in trouble but doesn't care, before sliding down his gym shorts. His thumbs are inside the band of his underwear when my neck whiplashes back around toward the sea.

Tops or bottoms first? It's like the worst of both worlds. I reach around and find the clasp, fiddle with it for an anti-erotic eternity. Then I feel Abram beside me. He takes my hand, at first like a father figure because I'm so tense, until I can loosen my fingers enough for him to slide his between them.

"Still counts," he says quietly, letting me know it's okay to cheat. "Kept my underwear on."

I let out the breath I've been holding and start walking forward with him, both of us making a point of looking straight ahead, as if there's no such thing as peripheral vision. How else could I see the curve of his calf muscle, the ridges of his quads, the V-shaped shadows pointing down toward his underwear? What does he see in me when there's literally nothing to see besides a two-dimensional blond stick with goose bumps?

If I were him, I'd be over me.

ABRAM

HER BEAUTY MULTIPLIES when she's vulnerable, makes her look like a beach angel who could drift off into the abyss if I'm not careful . . . hence the dogged persistence of my hand-holding. The majority of my focus is on not letting her become a danger to herself, as it should be; the rest is on making sure things don't get too prominent down yonder. For once, I'm looking forward to the physiological effects of freezing water. It's not like I'm trying to get on her in the Atlantic. All I really want is the chance to kiss her, whether that's on land or in ocean, naked or clothed, makes no difference, not picky.

"I can't feel my lower extremities," she says.

"That's not good. We can go back whenever."

The appreciation flashing in her green eyes sparks my imagination, inspires it to read too much into things: *Dude, look at the way her lips are parting, her head tilting to the side like she's seeing you as her significant other for the first time—is it just me, or does she want you to kiss her?*

Juliette

I COULD KISS HIM for that let's-go-back suggestion . . . to be continued, again. My teeth have to stop chattering first.

"Doesn't count until we're swimming," I say, dumbly wading onward, looking around for an iceberg we could float out on.

Hard to fathom why he's waited so long for a measly make-out session with this, especially considering how many sluts there are in the sea. Would it kill me to be a whore for two seconds? Never mind, I'm dying, because we've reached the part where we actually have to support ourselves without walking. And now we're kicking, floating, arms circling as our circulation cuts off, looking at each other and wondering what's next. I swim closer, an inch or two away from his face, trying to steal some of the steam rising from his head. He's attempting to be respectful by not pressing up against me, yet still keeping his skin close enough to keep mine as warm as possible. How did he know that's his new job? The blue in his eyes is darker than usual, the ink of his pupils having taken over, blind in their mission to make the most of this misadventure all about me. And that really does make me want to do something interesting for him in return. I'm getting there, I've stopped shivering, our lips are as close as they've ever been . . . and that's when I feel it . . . not Abram . . . a sea creature *gnawing at my foot.* I scream for my life—funny how much I suddenly care about it—then I groan for my death, because it's going to be a stupid one featured on *Shark Week,* with bittersweet commentary from surviving loved ones. I can count on my dad's refusal to be interviewed, but Heidi will cave and tell them everything, as will Abram's aunt Jane, because that lady sounds like she was born to do shows in need of fringe opinions. . . .

Abram is repeating my name, waving his hand in front of my face to get my attention. "That was my foot," he says, and it finally registers. I reach down to feel my leg, make sure there isn't a hammerhead attached to it, and . . . I've just had a far-death experience. We're laughing, practically fused together, as we swim to shore.

It's nice to have the last laugh be about something funny, not final.

ABRAM

WASN'T JUST MY IMAGINATION. Definitely should've kissed her.

24

Juliette

RUNNING—THE HOUR UNGODLY, the sun barely up. It's just me on this stretch of beach, and the sand is solid enough to keep my ankles from breaking, so those are two positives making it harder to complain about how I can't sleep in South Carolina, either, for instance. Meanwhile, Abram's still unconscious on the couch bed, recovering from his wild night with the new Juliette. That version is a *nightmare*, too.

Which is why I've downloaded a self-help audiobook from the black cloud that stores files above my iPhone. The title is *Silence Speaks*, and what can I say besides it spoke to me? The message is very Buddhist in nature, meaning the author sure does love trees and each short chapter is punctuated by the plunk of a single raindrop. He frequently encourages me to "be still" (can't, running) and process my surroundings "without attaching a label to everything" (not realistic). I wonder what he'd say about this mid-run pill I'm about to take? Probably something like, *Is it you who thinks you need that pill, or is that your ego-run mind telling you a story about how Juliette, the girl who's on Adderall, is due for her next one?* My response to all this is to continue dry-swallowing the pill, but be a tinge more conflicted about it than usual. At the same time, the seagulls increase their cawing overhead, guffawing at how little I'm progressing, the desperate measures I'm taking by listening to this spiritual guru turn each sentence into something I want to be over halfway before he finishes.

"Remain present," he says zenly. "Don't let your life be run by the illusion of time. Quit examining the past for clues to your identity, looking to the future for your salvation."

Know who doesn't need an audiobook to remind him not to check his watch every other second? Abram. He doesn't wear a watch; often forgets his cell phone in his car because it's perpetually slipping out of his pocket, and still finishes the nothing he's been doing once he realizes it's gone. Just another one of life's challenges he's conquering better than I am by putting forth the minimal amount of effort.

"Where's the nearest Starbucks?" I yell out to one of my best friends, startling the cute, old-ladyish runner I'm sprinting past. She points to her earmuff-sized headphones, thinking I was asking her; I point to my phone and mouth *Siri*. This doesn't clear up the confusion, but she cares as much as I do about getting to the bottom of it, which is very little. I love her like an ancestor.

I veer off to the left, looking for the nearest yard to cut through.

• • •

I just ordered an iced coffee for Abram. What does that mean? I don't know, but the green Starbucks straw complements his blue eyes, giving the flecks of kindness in them something to bounce off besides the emerald void of my irises.

"Can I have your name, please?" the Starbucks barista asks in the squeaky voice of a former Olympic gymnast.

"Sorry?"

"Your name?"

Starbucks' customer-personalization policies aren't—looking at her name tag—Janette's fault, but I don't see anyone from corporate to blame. Deep breath, calm down, remain present, what would Abram do? He'd answer her. Maybe even ask how brutal her day has been so far.

"Angela," I inform her.

Janette's marker squeaks across the side of my drink as she writes it. "You *do* kind of look like an Angie."

Gross!

"I don't really go by Angie," I say, because Angela is one of those defensive girls who's spent her entire life fighting the shortened version of her name—she's awful, but I could relate to what she's been through if people tried to call me Julie or, please never, Jules.

"No worries," the barista says with a *What is she on?* look on her face that makes me like her more. I smile and wink like I was totally joking.

"You staying on the island long?"

"Yuck. Do I look like a tourist, Janette?"

She smiles. "Not at all. You have *that glow* about you."

I hold up my arm, re-examining my stark-white tan.

"Ha, you know what I mean," Janette says, like we're in on something juicy together.

"Sorry, I don't."

"Is the lucky guy here with you?" she whispers, looking around the café.

I shake my head slowly, then force myself to acknowledge what she's been getting at. "Still passed out on the couch, unfortunately."

"Where'd y'all meet?"

"Oh, you know, we were both *in the neighborhood*," I say, and there's a throaty, womanly quality to my voice that catches us both off guard. It's *the her* in me—kind of similar to when Kate Hudson suddenly sounds exactly like Goldie Hawn, but without their relatable qualities and unbreakable mother-daughter bond.

"Hello?" I say into my cell. It's Siri. I make a regretful face to Janette, pointing to the phone like I have to take this call. She hands me a drink carrier and waves me away like these sorts of interruptions happen all the time. I'm grabbing a napkin to wrap around Abram's iced coffee at the drink-doctoring station I typically avoid, when I feel her eyes back on me, if they ever even left. There's something else in them besides curiosity, which has absolutely no business being there: my business.

25

ABRAM

JULIETTE'S STANDING over the couch bed with her arms crossed, dressed in a pair of tight black workout pants and a matching black long-sleeve. No clue what time it is, but she's about to tell me what I'm late for.

"We're going for a run," she says with extra intensity, handing me an iced coffee. Unexpected bonus: She's already put the straw in for me. I take the water-beaded cup from her hand, thanking her, trying not to drain it in one gulp as she watches me bring the straw to my lips for three mini-chugs in a row.

She pulls back the blankets from my chin. "Is that what you're wearing?"

I'm in my boxer briefs. Thankfully, nothing's escaped or excited or arranged at an odd angle. I sit up and start looking around the floor for the same clothes I wore last night. She points to the overstuffed chair next to the fireplace, having already laid out a clean pair of shorts, a T-shirt, and

socks. She also found the remote control to the fireplace, because the flames are crackling. Through the window behind it, the sun is rising above the water.

"Don't put on your shirt yet." She walks over and starts spraying me down with enough sunscreen to make the ozone a moot layer. Not that I'm complaining, especially when she starts rubbing the spray gently into my neck, as liberally as she's ever done anything when it comes to touching me. She even remembers the backs of my ears.

A short while later, we're on the beach, running, and it doesn't suck as much as I recalled, but I'm sure sucking a lot of air.

"You okay?" Juliette asks, with plenty of breath to spare.

I nod.

"Adderall?" she offers, as casually as one would an Advil. "I keep an extra underneath the insert of my shoe."

Once I realize she's not kidding, I shake my head no, and she looks at me like it's my loss. Except it's not, I tell her, because that tiny chunk of pill she gave me a few weeks ago, before eighth period, made my brain latch on to all kinds of to-do's: *Abram! You should make a bunch of lists and clean your locker and pick scabs that turn out to be freckles and trim your fingernails, but it's essential that you do this all at the same time!*

I consider anything related to me wanting to multitask a disorienting, what's-happening-to-me? experience, and on that note, I should make sure I don't step on a one-hundred-thousand-dollar sea-turtle egg.

"Can we take a break soon? Just a thought."

She checks her iPhone. "It's only been twenty-eight minutes and thirty-three seconds."

I grab her hand and lead her back toward the house. Break time. She's been needing to give herself one for a while now, anyway.

Juliette

ABRAM DOESN'T SEEM to have a plan, but he *does* find the exact spot of sand I would've chosen—a good distance away from that demented scene over there: a visibly happy couple making a sand castle with their bouncy, halterkini-wearing little girl. The two of us sit down, and then nothing happens. At least the sun feels like it's burning the pale off my face, since I've stopped moving long enough to let it get a decent shot. *Remind me why you quit running again?* asks my brain, but instead of waiting for an answer, it releases a few more stress hormones. I'd worry about my health if I weren't the type of lifeless person who lives forever. Guaranteed, I'll be five hundred years old someday, the stereotypically bitter old lady down the road who refuses to croak out of spite toward people long since dead, and all I'll have to show for my life is a bunch of check marks. *Remember that one time I went to the beach with a cute boy, completed a bunch of self-given assignments, and vacuumed the fun out of everything? Granny would never admit to regretting that, so let's talk about something you're doing wrong.* I won't have any kids or grandchildren lighting candles around my deathbed, though, so I'll just be lecturing my hospice nurse, mistaking her for my next of kin as she yearns to pull the plug.

The above out-of-control thought sequence is exactly what my new audiobook warns against.

"What do you think about just hanging out here for a while?" Abram asks.

"Okay," I say, letting him do the thinking. He looks surprised. I wonder how long it will take him to realize this would be better with towels.

ABRAM

WE'RE RELAXING ON THE BEACH, sprawled out side by side on the towels we just fetched, without a responsibility in the world besides all the ones we're putting off back home. Juliette keeps asking if she's tan yet, holding out her arm for my "brutally honest opinion." To be honest, we've only been lying still for twenty minutes, but I prop myself up on my towel so I can better assess her pigmentation. Eventually, my eyes wander over to her smooth, taut stomach with its tiny little belly button that I'd like to do a shot of something out of someday, even if it's saltwater, and what was her question?

"You're at least as tan as me," I confirm.

She sighs. "I want to be as tan as you two years ago."

"Ah-ha, so you *did* see me as you were running by the courts pretending to ignore my shirtlessness."

I'm guessing the *W* she draws in the sand next to me stands for *Whatever.*

She sits up and takes off her sunglasses, looking over at me. "Not that it matters, but I could never tell who was winning . . . you were both so good."

"Dad usually won in practice."

"What about in a match?"

I hesitate. Feels almost like a betrayal to show off my bragging rights, tout my official tournament victories over my dad or whatever—the last of which was on this exact island, at the club across the street, after we won the doubles together. I confess my guilt about this to Juliette, and she reminds me he would've been a lot more upset if I'd let him win. Very true.

"I want to see you play again," she says.

"Naw, we should just take it easy this afternoon." When she responds by putting her sunglasses back on, I sit up straighter and remove mine. "You've already scheduled something, haven't you?"

She puts her hand over her heart in a sarcastic gesture of innocence, then tells me we have four o'clock reservations at the club across the street.

26

Juliette

"WHEN'S THE LAST TIME you played?" Abram asks as we step out onto the court together.

"Can't remember," I say, like it's the funniest thing. It's not—I took a few mother-daughter tennis lessons a year and a half ago. Mom's idea. Her bribing me with Adderall was mine. I spent most of my time on court making snarky comments under my breath about Mom's sudden interest in the sport. I remember hitting exactly one forehand when we were playing doubles together—the ball only smacked the back of her arm, but in that particular moment of resentment, it felt like my first Wimbledon title.

"What about you?" I ask Abram.

He pops the lid off a can of tennis balls, tearing off the metal seal. "Here . . . last year," he says, then bends over and starts tying his shoes. I recognize more and more of our surroundings from the picture on Abram's refrigerator—the one of him and his father holding a trophy.

Maybe I should stretch a bone or two? I grab my phone, reach down, and touch my toes, letting the blood rush to my head as I send Heidi a text asking for some last-minute tips. Her immediate response of *Get it!!!* is not relevant, but it's incredible how she keeps finding a way to use the phrase, regardless of the context. Do I have to give her props for that? Anyway, it was nice of her to let me re-borrow the Maria Sharapova dress I wore to her party. This time, though, I'm pairing it with Chris Evert's frosty eye daggers. The look is vintage bitchy couture. As for Abram, he's dressed in the same pocket T-shirt he probably would've worn if we'd just sat back at the house staring at each other, although the shorts he's wearing are a bit shorter than his others, his legs looking tanner and therefore more muscular by the minute.

We walk back to our respective baselines, and this surface underneath my feet . . . Abram calls it "green clay," but it's basically a bunch of tiny rocks that hop up into the backs of my shoes whenever I take a step. Abram's already sliding around like he's rediscovering his childhood sandbox, which is exactly what he should be doing.

"Ready?" he calls out, his voice echoing off the tall backstop behind him.

"Yes. No, sorry, hang on. . . ." My grip feels weird, slippery. Need to get in my ready position, which is the same as my other ramrod stance only with a light swaying back and forth like I'm about to produce some tennis. I signal for Abram to bring it on. The ball pops off his racquet, spinning, spinning, landing a few inches in front of me and bouncing three feet higher than expected. My racquet connects with the ball, but I'm not even sure where I hit it.

Abram apologizes in spite of it actually being my fault, then sends another try my way.

ABRAM

About three rallies into the warm-up, Juliette complains of cold-wrist problems, which is a cover story for her being embarrassed about nailing her last shot straight past the baseline, into the backstop. She removes a sweatshirt from her purse and puts it on. She looks good in it. There's something about a girl like her in my hoodie: It doesn't fit, but it just fits.

She puts her tennis scowl back on and jogs to the baseline. I hit the next ball to her, and I can tell she's relieved when it brushes across her strings and bounces right back to me. She forgets to follow through, so I start exaggerating the correct path of the racquet after I make contact, thinking maybe she'll pick up on my technicalities. She does—in a sarcastic way that actually ends up improving her stroke—so mission accomplished. We rally for a few minutes longer until she starts walking up to the net with her hands on her hips. She might be defaulting. I trot up to join her.

"Everything okay?"

She rests her racquet on her hip, looking down at mine. "Are you really left-handed?"

"Nope, I'm fake left-handed," I say with a smile, using one of her favorite words to call people out with. "I write with my right hand, play sports with my left. Could've gone either way, but Dad thought I should be a lefty."

"Because he wanted you to have the ad-court advantage?" she asks. Not sure why I'm surprised she knows the game that well, given her close friendship with Heidi and formidable online research skills.

"Pretty much, yeah," I say, hitting the clay off the bottoms of my shoes with the edge of my racquet, just like he used to do.

"That was . . . awesome of him," she says, surprising herself. "Smart."

"Yeah . . . it was." For a second, I think about all the additional hours my dad must've spent teaching me to be left-handed. It frees me up to appreciate him and not feel guilty about it, or retroactively protective of my mom. "Thank you for saying that," I tell Juliette.

We hit for the next hour, during which she keeps telling me to stop making her look better than she really is by placing the ball in her strike zone every time. I can only do so much, as the uncoordinated ladies at the country club back home, where I taught a few summers ago, can attest. Unlike them, Juliette has athletic ability when she lets it come naturally, when she's just hitting the ball, letting her string tension do the work instead of the tension in her shoulders, and not analyzing her shot as it heads over the net. This is why tennis can be therapeutic for people sometimes: It requires you to problem-solve but doesn't leave enough time to overthink.

"I'd recognize that lefty forehand from a mile away!" a booming voice calls down to the court.

I look up to find a couple of ghosts from my tennis past, staring down at me from the stands.

27

Juliette

ABRAM WAVES UP at our unexpected visitors, a mask of anxious politeness freezing over his face. Isn't that the same mask I wore when cornered at Starbucks earlier? I'm going to need it back if he expects me to make a friendly impression on that Brawny-paper-towel-of-a-man who keeps pulling up his shorts. Incredible how the petite brunette seems to love him anyway—maybe forgiveness is easier to generate with a heart-shaped face like hers? The width of her smile certainly appears effortless.

"We'll come up and say hi," Abram tells them. He jogs around the net post to my side, takes my hand. "Terry and Linda McEvans," he says into my ear. "Neighbors, love tennis, used to hang out with my parents."

"Did they hang out with *our* parents?" I whisper.

"Not that I know of."

As we walk up the stairs, I really want to blame him for us being in this situation. If only it weren't my fault for making the reservation. When we reach the top, I take a small step in the opposite direction, hoping elsewhere is still an option. Abram calmly herds me back in tandem with him.

"I told Terry to wait till y'all were done," the woman says as we approach them, "but the doctor said he can't help it if he's chronically obnoxious."

"Doc's right, I'm untreatable!" Terry says proudly, twitching his mustache. "And 'bout had myself a heart attack when I saw the name Abram Morgan on the court assignment calendar." He looks at Abram with squinty-eyed amusement. "How you hitting 'em these days, champ? We has-beens want to know."

"Infrequently," Abram says too honestly, smiling. I would've gone with a lie/frown combo.

"That's *not* what I like to hear," Terry says good-naturedly, and he and Abram begin working their way through a complicated handshake-hug-handshake ritual. Linda shakes her sleek nightly-newscaster hair back and forth like she doesn't understand it, either, before fixing her energetic brown eyes on me.

"Hi, I'm Linda McEvans. Terry and I live just down the road from the Morgans." She has the kind of duskily feminine voice that cracks at all the right times, with just a hint of southern twang.

"Your neighborhood is very nice," I say, in the voice of an alien who doesn't vacation on Earth very often. "I'm Juliette."

Terry extends his furry paw and introduces himself to me, saying, "The pleasure is all mine, Juliette." Indeed, but I like how his grip is loose and unassuming; firm handshakes are overrated.

Terry stands back and picks up Abram's racquet, takes a few imaginary practice swings. "I know I don't look like much now," he says to anyone who'll listen, "but I used to play a lot of competitive tennis in my day. And you know who forced me into my third or fourth retirement?" He points to Abram. "Last year's version of this guy."

"Don't beat yourself up, I retired pretty much right after that tournament myself," Abram says.

Terry McEvans has more restraint than my snap judgment gave him credit for, because he doesn't ask why, just reaches out and pats Abram's shoulder like he's been there, quit that.

"You mind if I take his forehand for a spin?" Terry asks me. "Five minutes is my max these days, promise."

"By all means," I say, awfully. What's next? *Be my guest? Spin away?* I hand Abram the racquet he let me borrow.

Terry whispers something into Abram's ear, making sure I hear the part about me being a "keeper." I like the honest part where he mumbles "If you've got the energy to keep catching her" better. Linda smacks him on the arm for it before they head back down to the court, leaving us ladies to a few minutes of small talk followed by a lifetime of never seeing each other again.

Linda sits down on the bleachers and pats the spot next to her. What if I acted like it was already taken? I sit down and wait for the questions to begin as she removes a huge canister of sunscreen from an elephantine purse that rivals mine in size. I want to ask where one can purchase such a tote monster, but I don't, because now we're unspoken purse rivals.

"I'm paranoid about sunscreen," she says, speaking my language, and then proceeds to lambaste herself with the coconut-scented spray. She passes the bottle to me casually, as she might to a friend she's been sharing with for years. I give my arms another thin coat.

"Do you mind if I use this on my legs, too?" I ask Linda.

"Of course not."

No wonder I'm so pale.

We watch as Terry feeds the first ball to Abram, who then hits it back a million times harder than when playing me. Abram glides into each of his shots, totally balanced, timing each movement perfectly, popping the ball right back to the same annoying location above Terry's head every time as a *thwooomp* sound echoes around the court.

"So much talent," Linda says, but not like it's a shame he's been wasting it—as if she, too, is mesmerized by what Abram can produce with an easygoing smile on his face. Linda McEvans could've been a model in a past life, provided she was about a foot taller in that one. She takes care of herself, too. I bet her bathroom is full of expensive face creams and firming serums I'd have a hard time not slipping into my purse. I'd bet she's like a Heidi, someone who gets prettier and prettier the more you get to know her, while I do the opposite.

She also has something on her mind. She's less obvious about what's eating her than Starbucks Janette, but it's in there somewhere, throbbing inside her temples, wanting me to acknowledge it.

ABRAM

JULIETTE SEEMS TO BE getting along okay up there with Linda. Then again her expression hasn't changed yet, so Terry's guess is as good as mine, and he's too busy having fun. His enjoyment is making it hard to wrap things up in five minutes. He laughs as my latest return lands right on the baseline, takes a bad bounce, and whizzes past him. Excuse my French, but it feels good to be hitting *le shit* out of his serve again. I'm surprised to find myself feeling this way, but I doubt Juliette is. She's known all along tennis is in my blood. My dad's way of communicating with me.

When we're done, Terry puts his beefy arm around my neck and says, nonchalantly, "I'll make a comeback if you do, champ."

"Maybe. Let's see how lame we pull up in the morning."

The two of us sit down on the bench. Terry pours a cup of water over his head and turns to me, forehead dripping. "You know your mom told us to check in on you, right?"

"I figured she might."

"Suzy loved watching you and Ian play tennis, Abram. I don't get the sense it's gonna bring back bad memories for her, should you someday decide to start kickin' everybody's ass again. But, hey, what do I know?" He yells up at Linda and asks her the same question. She rolls her eyes and asks if he needs any ibuprofen.

"One more game?" Terry asks, nodding his head yes for me.

Juliette

ABRAM AND TERRY are shaking hands, having just finished a game called Butt's Up that they asked our permission to play. Now Terry's going back to the service line, bending over, and sticking his butt into the air. "Give me what I deserve!" he shouts. Linda groans and then laughs as Abram runs back to the baseline, prepares to take aim. He deliberately skims the ball just past Terry, who proceeds to fall down like he's been hit anyway.

"Did Abram's father ever bring another woman around?" I ask Linda quietly.

Linda turns to me, and she may be the definition of an unflappable Southern woman who's either been through it all herself or heard it all before, but her smile doesn't show as seamlessly this time.

"You mean your mother, hon?"

My fingers tighten around the edge of my seat. "So you met her?"

"We saw them here playing tennis a few times, had dinner with them once," she admits guiltily. "She was enchanting, your mother. The life of the party. Terry and I tried not to judge—we're certainly no angels ourselves—but of course it was hard not to think of Suzy and . . . everyone else involved."

Before I can apologize, Linda goes on to eulogize how sorry she is for my loss. The words don't sound quite as depressing in her southern accent, but I still feel like I'm attending another funeral. When she's not paying attention, I shoot Abram a look like we should *really* be going soon.

ABRAM

On our way out of the club, Terry and Linda offer to give us a ride home in their pimped-out golf cart. Juliette's fingers find their way to the skin on the back of my arm, pinching a *no* into it. I wonder if I'll ever learn what her *yes* signal feels like. Terry tries to make it happen by touting the cart's satellite radio and playing us a sample song, but all he gets me is pinched in the exact same spot.

"They're pretty nice, eh?" I say to her, when their golf cart has buzzed far enough away.

"Yes," Juliette says, "but I never want to see them again."

She's said this about a lot of people, of course—me, that happy family at the beach this morning, old teachers we pass in the hallway who'd love to keep in touch. She always means it, but this time she's got some extra oomph behind it.

28

Juliette

"EVER NOTICED HOW TIRED being at the beach makes you?" Abram asked me earlier tonight. "Not really," I said, then he called his mom, I started e-mailing my dad, and he passed out on our couch bed twenty minutes later, the end.

Now not only am I alone with my thoughts again—they're telling me it's my own fault for "going there" with Linda—I'm sore from tennis and starving. This popcorn isn't cutting it; not when I'm *craving*—can't believe I'm admitting this to myself—a Doritos Locos Supreme.

There's hope.

His eyelids are twitching.

"Abram."

No response.

"Taco Bell?"

Nothing.

I move my laptop station closer to him, lean over until my face is nearly touching his. It's warmer down here by his mouth, just as I suspected, maybe even anticipated on my worst days. I should've made it easier for him to kiss me in the ocean last night. His lips look firm, a little on the chapped side but in an intriguing way that makes sense for a boy; otherwise, I'd just make out with Heidi every once in a while and call it a phase. Bizarre that his breath hasn't offended me once since we met—must be his candy-flavored toothpaste. His lids twitch again, but he still doesn't open his eyes. His lashes are even longer from this close up. That's sort of interesting. Eventually, I manage to pull myself away from him. I don't go far.

ABRAM

I OPEN MY EYES, relieved to see Juliette hasn't fled to jog off her insomnia yet; in fact, she's maybe a little closer to my side of the bed than when I started dozing.

"Hi," she says softly, and I can see she's still typing the same e-mail to her dad on my laptop. So far, she's written *Hello, Dad: How's the new novel? Have you gotten up from your swivel chair since I left? Are you and the Keurig getting along? <Insert something like "I miss you" without actually saying it here.>* And that's all. Writer's block must run in the family.

"Hey there."

She minimizes the e-mail, turns toward me, and everything about her is more exotic and hypnotic than it's ever been. I think this pretty much every time she makes eye contact with me, but today her face seems a bit fuller and healthier than it's been this past year, possibly due to her increased exposure to my snacks. To this point, there's an open bag of popcorn beside her. I'm pleased that she a) helped herself to my stash, b) hasn't apologized for it yet, and c) curtailed the Adderall enough today to allow hunger to resume its rightful spot in her empty stomach.

Emboldened by my sleepy state, I reach over and pull her closer to me, against me, and she doesn't object or eject herself from the bed. In fact, she gets under the covers, finds the perfect position for almost every part of her body to connect with mine as I loop my arms around her and find her hands. Just like that, there's no such thing as a problem in my world.

"I brought up my mom to Linda. Mistake."

"What did she say?"

"That they hung out with our parents once, and she felt bad for your mom. I thought I could handle it, but it just . . . made me feel guilty by association. Which is ridiculous because I barely associated with my mom, especially toward the end; she was like a roommate I drank coffee with occasionally, a shady friend who gave me Adderall and disappeared all day, and I wish I was making sense."

"You're making a lot of sense," I say.

"It's been over a year, and I still don't understand how I'm supposed to be dealing with this, and I'm sick of taking Adderall but too tired to figure out how not to, and . . . I want a Doritos Locos Supreme but I can't even drive myself to Taco Bell."

"Why didn't you say something?"

She's shaking now. I roll her over to face me. Instead of trying to hide the tears in her eyes, she lets them do their thing right in front of me. I resist the urge to kiss them from her skin, because she probably wouldn't hate anything more. Instead, I graze her cheek with the side of my fingertip and slide them away, nonchalantly, as if only so she won't have to worry about clogged pores.

"Sorry," she says, sniffling, "I'm the world's ugliest crier."

"Or its reigning prettiest," I suggest as an alternative, which makes her cry harder for some reason. Time to rely on something other than words—take the action I've been meaning to take since CVS. I realize it's not a solution to anything, but it's the only thing I know will keep me from shedding a few tears myself, and then we'd really have ourselves a legitimate dude contender for the world's-ugliest-crier competition. And no one wants that.

29

Juliette

MY CRYING HAS SLOWED, thankfully, but the ugly won't be evacuating my face anytime soon. What's with the strange look of determination coming across Abram's? It's not going anywhere, either. Haven't seen an eyebrow furrow of this magnitude since his last beer-pong rematch.

ABRAM

NOT EVEN A WHALE jumping out of the ocean and swallowing the house could stop me from kissing her. Still don't want to take any chances, though, so now I'm rushing in a little faster than I would if I had a reciprocation guarantee. I slow down as I reach the very edge of her lips, and then finally, after all this time that seems longer than it's probably been, I close the deal. Our lips are touching, we're kissing, and I get to feel what she really feels like. So far she seems relaxed, eyes closed, not open and wondering how she landed herself in such a bind. I make every second count, not by overdoing it, by just experiencing her as much as possible—the softness of her lips, the smoothness of her other exposed areas when they brush up against me accidentally—without preconceived notions of how this miracle of all miracles should be unfolding.

Two peas in a couch bed. That's what we are.

Juliette

HIS LIPS STILL GRAZING MINE, Abram opens his eyes to make sure I'm okay with all this. I pull myself closer to him, careful not to respond with a mixed signal. His mouth presses down against mine more firmly, finding the perfect spot between my lips, our tongues touching briefly, shyly, before retreating to their respective corners. They don't stay away long. We repeat these movements in a slightly different way that feels entirely new every time. Then, unexpectedly, his face drifts down toward my neck. His lips know where to find the most sensitive part, the best possible area they can linger, and he kisses me there, intense and focused, channeling all his energy into this small, insignificant part of me. I give up on trying to keep his wavy hair out of his face and close my eyes, my breathing encouraging him to stay there as long as he feels like it or until I get weird. I lose track of everything, the sounds we're making, how long we've been doing this, where I'm positioning my legs and arms . . . until I accidentally touch his butt region.

ABRAM

HELLO THERE, was that a butt touch? Probably an accident. This is lasting about forty times longer than expected, which is great, no need to ever stop on my account. Might be time to mix it up again, keep her engaged. I pull away from her neck just long enough to make her wonder, and then move back in toward her lips, at a different angle, before she can figure me out.

This might be too bold, but I lift myself up and maneuver around until I'm on top of her, still supporting my weight on my elbows. Managing to do this without my lips leaving hers. I hope she doesn't think I'm expecting to jump immediately from kissing to bootytown; I just really needed to move my hip off the spring from the couch bed that's been digging into it.

Juliette

ON TOP OF MY BODY is certainly not where I thought he was going with this. The situation still doesn't seem out of hand, the claustrophobia yet to kick in. He's not making any pained expressions about my hipbones stabbing into his kidneys, either, so that's considerate of him. Should I rub his back so he doesn't suspect I'm a closet butt fetishist? I never know what to do with my hands in these physical-intimacy scenarios, maybe because they never occur, and, yes, Heidi, this includes when I'm alone. *Get it!* she calls out from a jail cell in my mind. I'll probably kiss and tell her about this, and when I do, I'll say

Abram's a great kisser and then I'll resist answering her animated follow-up questions that will center around length and girth. Or is all of the above not the point of anything?

Eventually, against all odds, I really start to relax, not just fake relax, and there's a marked shift in the way my lips operate. They're more confident in their throbbing pursuit of Abram's. Throbbing is a gross word, but that's what they're doing, like they've been starving for this all along, and now that they've gotten a taste, they can't get enough. I put my hand on his lightly stubbled face, wondering how I'm going to force myself to stop. Then my body makes the decision for me.

"Can we go to Taco Bell in five minutes?" I ask.

Abram smiles. "I'm so happy your stomach growled that up again."

An hour later, Abram thinks I should try driving in the Taco Bell parking lot.

"Bad idea," I say, grimacing like I wish it'd been a good one.

He shakes his head, undeterred. "It's just like riding a bike."

"I hate bikers."

"Ah, that's right—bad example. Just do a loop around here. You don't have to go on the main road." He gestures toward the sea of empty parking spaces. (Behind us, hungry patrons form a desperate horseshoe of cars around the twenty-four-hour drive-thru lane.)

"You should've asked me before that happened," I say, pointing to the bag full of empty Doritos Locos Supreme wrappers.

"Tacos can only help matters. Look at me, I eat a lot of them, and I'm a pretty good driver, no?"

He's a great driver, actually, but that has nothing to do with me getting out of this. Or here's a crazy thought: I could just do it, say yes, try something new again. What's so hard about trading Abram spots, taking the wheel, and parking right next to the space we're in?

I unlock the door and step out into a small swarm of no-see-ums, which really are worse than mosquitoes, it's not just some boring thing people say to hear themselves sounding fascinated about nature. Anyway, bad omen. I slam the door and run around toward Abram's side. I tell him to get back in through his side, and he does, sliding over into the passenger seat as I shut the door behind me. In full teammate mode, Abram makes a fist-bump request with his balled hand outstretched, and for some reason I bump it. It makes me feel dumber, but better.

It's actually not overwhelming in the driver's seat, especially in park, in Abram's tank of an SUV. I like that I'm up high, that if I accidentally accelerated directly into a car like that Hyundai Elantra over there it wouldn't result in my vehicle losing control and plummeting down a steep ravine. Because, wouldn't you know, there's always a steep ravine nearby when I get into hypothetical car accidents.

I adjust the rearview mirror, then check it to see if I've grown at all as a person. Not yet. Abram wisely buckles up and points to the widget that I'm supposed to shift from P to D. It's not responding. Something's off.

Abram reminds me, without judgment, that I may want to push down on the brake first. I laugh and try reversing again. Watch out, America. I circle the parking lot over and over again, Abram saying "Maybe you don't want to get *that* close" after I graze the edge of a bush, and "You're speeding up when someone pulls into the drive-thru as a joke, right?" he asks, as I fail to realize that's what I'm doing. He's the only kind of teacher I can learn from. I'm still a danger to myself and anything in my path—e.g., the empty soda cup I just ran over—but I feel my world expanding by just the slightest of margins.

30

ABRAM

JULIETTE AWAKENS THE NEXT MORNING to an unlikely role reversal: me, fully dressed, staring down at her with two Starbucks cups in my hands. She thanks me and accepts the drink before vowing never to let me "beat her up again." I assure her I'm a lover, not a fighter.

She takes a couple of sips, then sits up straighter. "Did you see Janette there?"

"Who?"

"Janette. The barista I was hating the other day."

"Oh, *that* Janette." I shake my head nope; I can barely remember driving there and back. Juliette's follow-up descriptions of Janette's "Kerri Strugg voice" and "suspicious leprechaun eyes" don't ring any bells for me, either. I must be too excited about today. . . .

"I have another surprise for you," I say, watching as the announcement hits her like a ton of bricks.

"Does it involve other people?"

"Technically, no. We depart in an hour."

An hour and a half, actually, but I don't want to leave her too much time to cancel back and forth with. The way I've set this up seems to be working . . . she's intrigued. If I'm not careful, I might turn into an accidental love genius.

Fifty-five minutes later, I'm showered and as ready as I'll ever be. Juliette? Showered, but she "might never be ready, sorry." Her words, and they'll come true if she keeps getting into fights with her hair. Every time she passes a reflective surface, she picks up where she left off, and then she's grabbing at the tie holding her bun in place and attempting to ramrod it smooth again. The southern humidity has other ideas—for instance, *How 'bout some curls instead, y'all?* It also has a southern accent.

"Isn't the beachy look popular with you girls these days?" I say, testing out my wavering grandpa voice.

Juliette smirks into the mirror and says, "You mean with those crusty girls who put gel in their hair, Grandpa?"

I take a gulp of my iced coffee, smack my lips, and say, as creepily as possible, "Grampy likes 'em a little crusty, heh-heh-heh."

Eventually she sits down on the chair across from me, accuses me of staring at her hair—which I don't deny, because it looks good.

"Are you sure us going through with this is necessary?"

"No loopholes," I say, removing the itinerary I folded too

many times from my pocket and spreading it out onto the coffee table. I have to hold it in place with a coaster so that it lies flat. Now I kind of know how she feels about her hair.

She speed-reads the contents of the paper, looks up at me. "A whale-watching expedition?"

"I was thinking we should go visit our distant relatives," I explain. She's quiet for a minute, but in a contemplative way, not a grouchy one. I bet she's thinking about that first night at my house, after CVS, how we talked about the whale versions of ourselves, the way things might've played out had we been born underwater.

"I tried to find a boat with Wi-Fi for you," I say, "but it's not really something they prioritize."

"Doesn't matter. This . . ." She rolls her eyes and looks away. For a second, I think she's disappointed, and then her entire face breaks out into a smile. She's never let it do that before. "This is one of my favorite things anyone's ever done for me."

"It is?"

"I have weird standards."

"Or," I say, "you have *whale* standards." Juliette seems to like this explanation better. She stands up and walks over to me, and suddenly her face is front and center, and I can feel each of her shallow breaths on my skin as she tilts her chin downward, till her lips are aligned with mine. She gives me the lightest of kisses. "Thank you," she says. I try not to behave myself, draw her back in with my animal magnetism, but she has to pack her purse. Don't think we need the remote control she just threw inside it accidentally, but I keep quiet, just sit there and smile until she comes back over with a can of sunscreen in her hand and tells me to take off my shirt. I whistle at the familiar thought of my own bare chest and then do as she demands. I know what's good for me. Her.

"Let me know if you see any 'whales,'" Juliette says with fingers crooked into skeptical air quotations. Then she reaches into her purse and pulls out her phone in hopes that its cellular data signal has strengthened. In this case, I don't blame her for trying to escape reality—would be doing the same if I hadn't left my phone in some other shorts pocket back at the house. With all due respect to the whales, watching them remain underwater is kind of a snoozer. Not that I expect them to be all *Yeah, we'll be right up, can't wait to see you, too!* given how many harpoons they've historically taken to the forehead.

"Wonder why they call them right whales," I say to Juliette.

"Because poachers deemed them the 'right whale' to hunt," she answers, like a human Siri. That must be from one of the articles she downloaded before we left shore. Her web research skills are stronger than ever, and I think I figured out why she's always honing them: because if she googles it, then she can separate herself from it; it becomes something "other" and turns into knowledge that can't sneak up on her. Anyway, I want her back in the same boat as me.

"Wanna play rock-paper-scissors?" I ask.

This seems to work every time, distracting her with

games, because she quickly puts away her phone, stretches her fingers for maximum dexterity, and then places her fist within the air between us. I do the same. She's probably thinking I'll pick rock, because that's the obvious boy choice, so I go with scissors. I lose, she pounds the crap out of my scissors with her rock. Then I pick scissors again, same result.

"Juliette," I say, grabbing her leg, pointing toward the large circles forming in the water to the left of the boat.

"Quit trying to throw off my rhythm with a fake whale-sighting," she says, blowing the gun smoke off her fist.

I really do think I'm spotting a whale, so I reach around and place my hand behind her back, sliding her across the slippery canvas seat until she's leaning into me and can see the water from my point of view.

"Oh my God," she whispers, as our fellow watchers crowd against the side of the boat.

We stare for I don't know how long, in awe, afraid to move, as if the whale is the equivalent of an easily spooked horse. She's not. She's much calmer than any of us.

"I need my phone," Juliette says, after a calf surfaces beside its mother.

"Not yet," I tell her—not pushily, just firmly, trying to convey that this is a moment to experience before gathering evidence of it. "Just watch with me for a few more seconds." I take her hand. She doesn't argue when I say a snapshot wouldn't do the whales justice anyway. I'd post it on Facebook and my former teammates would leave comments like *Cool, dude, but where's the face?* Or my aunt Jane would say, *You sure that's not your shadow, Abram? Guess this means another six weeks of winter!* Not worth it. Plus that Hawaiian-shirted guy with the high-powered camera around his neck promised to e-mail his pictures to us.

After the whales are gone, we settle into a did-that-just-happen? window of time. Juliette is completely free of thought. I can tell because she's really looking at me, not through me or around me, trying to find the answer to something without having to ask me for it. In this moment, in these surroundings, I'm more than enough for her, and I don't even have to convince her no one's looking as I lean in close.

"It feels like home out here," I say, a millimeter farther from her face than I'd like to be. She smiles at me with her eyes before my lips press against hers.

31

ABRAM

Juliette and I are in our couch bed underneath the same fourteen blankets, pillows propped, my arm wrapped around her. I really wish she wouldn't insist on making this happen, especially after we've just eaten so much sweet-and-sour kitty from the Chinese takeout place. The act just seems hasty, at least by her methodical standards—like something she might regret for the rest of her senior year.

I can't deny that a very large part of me wants her to go through with it, nor can I emerge from my rice coma long enough to stop her from polishing up my dashboard with a wad of napkins. Now she's stretching her wrists, cracking her neck back and forth, preparing to take action regardless of what anyone else thinks. Her face is getting paler, her breathing more ragged, and she looks like I do right before I release food back into the universe involuntarily.

"You don't have to do this," I tell her.

"I know."

Juliette

I'M NERVOUS, half-tempted to pray for the best—does God accept sarcastic texts from people he's never heard from? Never mind, it's just that I haven't done this in *so long*. Is it really so impossible to show Abram he exists to me, in a meaningful way, by cheapening our relationship on Facebook? *Yes*. Posting imagery that proves we hang out together in our spare time is the ultimate sacrifice, right up there with the awkward sex we won't be having tonight.

I log in to my account and wince at the Jerseylicious profile picture staring back: me, sophomore year, wearing too much bronzer and a noticeably fatter face.

"Hey, you look hot in that pic," Abram says. I'll delete it later, after I complete what I came here to do: upload a picture of Abram and me from earlier today. Sans whales, unfortunately, because Abram was right—as far as whale-watching goes, you have to be there. Case in point, my best snapshot looks like I threw my gray cable-knit scarf into the ocean trying to pass it off as a whale, which isn't above me. Glad I didn't, though, because otherwise said scarf wouldn't be keeping my neck toasty right now.

It should be noted what I'm about to post isn't just any pic. It's an f'ing selfie! A few minutes ago, Abram and I held a competition over who could think of the best name for a couple's selfie. His: couplet, twosie, double-header. Mine: cheesie, stankjob, lamepeg. He deserved to win. Unfortunately, he didn't—I disqualified him.

If I look too closely at the pixels, like I am now, I can barely recognize myself as the wavy-haired, semi-tanned, de-stressed damsel who's lucky to be there, watching whales with Abram's arm around her, especially after lodging as many complaints as I did about the surprise. No wonder I want so badly to share this with seven hundred people I never talk to. *Look how functional I suddenly am again, everyone!* No one's going to Like it.

ABRAM

THAT'S A PRETTY GOOD-LOOKING COUPLET, if I do say so myself. Juliette's all worried about the inherent selfie-ness of the image, but my long arm got us a pretty sweet angle, and you can't even tell. Now she's trying to maneuver the thumbnail around the upload box so that the image displays as little of her body as possible. She calls it "being considerate of others," but I call it a "thirty percent loss of a nice, tight body." I agree to disagree; she doesn't.

Click.

The picture goes live.

She turns to me, placing her fingers to her lips. "What have I done?"

I sit up and try to kiss her frown upside down through her fingers. I'm not successful.

Juliette

I STARE AT OUR POSTED PICTURE, willing someone to Like us. No one does, which is what I get for not being likable. Social media is all about reciprocity—I'll Like your newborn baby with the misshapen head if you Like this depressing picture I just scanned of my unsmiling great-great-grandparents, etc.—and that's not a back-and-forth I felt capable of participating in until about twenty-four hours ago, when Abram first kissed away some of the grouchy fug from my face.

It's been at least ten seconds and the picture is already plummeting down people's newsfeeds. I'll give it thirty more seconds before I gladly pay Facebook ten dollars to promote it back up to the top. I tag Abram, hoping to bottom-feed a few Likes from his four-digit Friend count, and then check my e-mail to see if my dad's written me back. I never finished my apology e-mail to him; got us a family subscription to Lumosity, the unnecessary brain-training website, and forwarded the notification along with a weird smiley face and a few warnings about not starting until his book is finished.

Huge relief to see his name back in my inbox where it belongs; his e-mail says the book is flowing and his brain is suddenly feeling much more flexible, even without the neuroscientific training he's now moderately addicted to. *I'm proud of you, Dad,* I type in response. Am I allowed to say this as his child? Have I ever cared about such boundaries? Send. Facebook no longer seems Like-or-Death.

But I still want to check our Like count one more time . . . click. Seven people have Liked it, including Heidi, who also commented: *If only I'd been there in the background photo-bombing you!!*

Oh, Heidi. Maybe I'll finally go to that Britney Spears concert she's been trying to drag me to for ten years—a trashy night on the town, just the two of us, would mean a lot to her. As I'm promising her this, via text, the last person on earth I'd expect to Like a picture of Abram and me pops up beside Heidi's name.

I was secretly hoping she'd Like us together.

32

ABRAM

I'M NOT SURPRISED my mom Liked our picture. She's a Facebook person. As well as a great person who doesn't sweat the small stuff and would never be like, *Appreciate the olive branch, but I think I'm going to hang on to my self-alienating thoughts of being wronged by you, thanks.* That's why she'll always have love for my dad, keep his picture around the house, wear a red mummy dress for him every once in a while. I used to worry that this was stopping her from moving on, but I realized, after playing tennis yesterday, that it's possible to have our fun and remember the good things about Dad, too.

Juliette moves the cursor over my mom's name and clicks the Add Friend button. Glad I stayed awake long enough to watch this day getting even better. She looks over at me, blushes, then jokingly checks my pulse to cover up her friendliness shame.

"I won't be offended when she doesn't accept."

"No need to not be offended," I say, struggling to be coherent. Doesn't matter, because Mom accepts a few seconds later, and it's the only time in my life I've wondered what we'd all do without Facebook. Because Facebook, at least in terms of my mom and Juliette right now, is a place to start.

Juliette

WATCH OUT, our picture is going viral. Fifty-plus people have Liked us so far, and I can't stop watching the numbers climb like I'm accomplishing something, even when a scary-looking woman with a pixie haircut and visible biceps veins tries to ruin my Facebook buzz with her comment: *Oh, my god, SO CUTE TOGETHER. When are you two coming over to my house for dinner??? I'll make my famous tofu lasagna!*

"Aunt Jane," Abram tells me, with one eye open.

I zoom in on her picture. "She means well?"

"That's what they say," he says. "That, and she doesn't take no for an answer." Then he sits up and kisses my nose—"Because I've never kissed it" is his rationale—before plopping back down and telling me to prepare for an aggressive Friend request.

I pretend I'm going to shut the laptop screen . . . then don't because I'm still watching the Likes. I accept Aunt Jane's request when it comes my way, have to laugh when she tags both Abram and me in her latest post, a Bible passage from 1 Corinthians, the "Love is patient, love is kind" thumper read at nearly every wedding ceremony by the bride or groom's favorite aunt. It's between Aunt Jane, my dad's estranged sister in Oregon, and an empty pulpit—tough one. Both of Abram's eyes are closed now, so I start reading, rewriting the words of 1 Corinthians in my head as I go.

*Love doesn't sigh impatiently. Love isn't "over it" before it even started. Love isn't like, "Does that Asian violinist have a nicer David Yurman bracelet than me? No, she definitely doesn't. Thank God—can you imagine?" Love doesn't thank God someone else has an inferior bracelet to make itself feel better. Love isn't sitting across the table from someone it cares about, wondering, "That's great about you and all, but what's in it for me?" Love isn't a loose cannon that's forever pointing to its short fuse in an attempt to scare others away. Love doesn't store throwaway comments in a safe place for reference during the next fight it picks. Love doesn't lie about how much Adderall it's taken or plans on taking in the future. Love protects its love object from harmful UVB rays, and too much junk food, and the selective serotonin reuptake inhibitors that are making him think mixing Ben & Jerry's Cookie Dough ice cream with Cool Whip is an acceptably edible food invention. Love has confidence in its love object; knows there's no reason to be suspicious, because clearly he's not going anywhere given how many times it's tried to push him away. Love doesn't become paranoid and evacuate the premises without letting its love object know the panic button has been struck. Love doesn't quit when the going gets awkward and overwhelming and it can't deal, the end. Love stays put when something disguised as "better" comes along. Love knows the difference between what's passing and what's permanent, even if it pretends it doesn't sometimes, just to see if its love object feels the same way.**

**Love realizes it shouldn't play games.*

I glance over at Abram and find him awake again, squinting through the artificial light of the laptop, smiling crookedly in my direction, like he suspects something but is too groggy to investigate. What if he was reading my mind that whole time?

"You want popcorn, too, don't you?" he says.

I raise an eyebrow and shake my head in wonderment, like, *Wow, I can't hide anything from you, can I?* I bet I look dumb right now. He slides out of the bed and pads off toward the microwave in his boxer briefs. You'd think he was fully dressed, like me, the way his arms and legs are so loose and nonchalant about so much of his body being on display. He really is a graceful mover, when he's actually in motion. I should be thinking of anything else, so I redirect my attention to the beeping and whirring of the microwave, the kernels popping, the accompanying aroma of "movie theater butter."

"Seriously, when are you going to admit you *love* popcorn?" Abram says when he returns with a steaming bag in hand.

"Probably never," I say. "Or maybe the same day you remember the napkins."

He gets back up.

Do I love Orville Redenbacher? Is that possible when we've only really known each other a month? I close the laptop and make myself wait a few seconds before eating any of his popcorn.

33

ABRAM

THE HURRICANE JULIETTE'S FATHER was worried about? Not on the radar, but it's raining like a mother this fine Sunday morning, our last full day here. I'm drinking a glass of emergency water just to see what the purifying tablets make it taste like. Juliette's sitting in the same chair as me, on my lap, the flame-retardant blanket draped over us. Just the two of us watching the raindrops fall into the ocean from the back deck.

"Still tastes exactly like water," I announce, holding out the glass for her to try. She takes my word for it and continues to sip from her coffee mug. So far today, she's taken one-fourth fewer Adderalls. It's a start . . . one she claims is making her tired.

"I wish we could do shots," she says wistfully. I pull the hood of my sweatshirt from her head to see if she's more serious than usual—can't tell, but I like this angle of her face, too.

"Where there's a will, there's a shot," I say in my deep voice, as if a wise frat brother once said the same.

"Yes, but there's no drive-thru. And there's the possibility of seeing Janette."

Got it, she must be talking about espresso shots at Starbucks.

"Remind me why this Janette lady's so evil again?"

"I never told you in the first place," she states, not like she's annoyed, just as a fact. "She's probably fine. She just had an eerie look on her face. The same one Linda had before I asked her about my mom."

I nod. "What if we just peer in through the windows, see if she's there?" I'm scratching her back because it's pretty much the only part of her I have unrestricted access to right now. "Then I'll go inside and be really stealthy about making sure the coast is clear."

She looks back at me. "Your plan . . . I kind of hate it."

"But it just might work?"

"Probably not," she says, "but let's try it."

We're hiding in the alley next to Starbucks while I reassure Juliette I've checked everywhere inside for an annoying lady with a Janette name tag. "Including the men's bathroom."

"Thank you." Juliette bites her lip. "What about the women's?"

"Occupied. And the occupant sounded like she'd be in there for a while."

"Let's leave before she's finished being disgusting," she says, as I hold the door open for her. There's no line at the cash register, which puts her in a better mood. Our drinks and shots are ready almost immediately, and we're about to leave when we look out the window and see the monsoon.

"You were right," she says. "We should've driven."

"Want to sit for a minute?" I ask—one of my other favorite suggestions.

She looks around for a nook or cranny. We head toward a table at the far corner of the room, near the fireplace, and rotate our chairs so we're facing away from an improbable Janette sighting. "I need to show you a few things," Juliette says, rummaging through the catacombs of her purse, "of yours. I stole them."

"Haven't been missing anything. . . ."

"I'm afraid you have."

She places a pile of envelopes on the table next to my iced coffee, along with a two-hundred-dollar receipt from the Salvation Army? Juliette wads up the receipt, says, "Don't you recognize your mail?"

Now that she mentions it. "Looks different without the dust," I say.

"You can be mad at me for violating your privacy. Promise I won't argue to make it seem like your fault."

"I'm sure you were just trying to help."

"Maybe. You should still consider hating me for a little while."

I raise my eyebrows, like, *Thought you weren't going to argue.* I tell her if I wanted to keep my mail top-secret, I should've read it a long time ago, rather than let it sit on my dresser for an eternity. Besides, it's not like she opened it or anything.

I pick up a letter with VIRGINIA TECH in the return-address space. Juliette frowns. "Sorry, I opened that one."

I turn the envelope around to examine the perfectly sealed back flap. "Where?"

She points to the corner. I nod, but I still have no idea how she got in without a rip. "You do good work," I tell her, and she's more accepting of this compliment than most of my others combined.

"Are you not going to college, or what?" she asks.

"What? Yeah, I'm going." I open the envelope halfway, stop. "I've just been . . . deferring the decision-making process."

"Until when? Someone else makes it for you?"

"Probably," I force myself to admit aloud, take the embarrassment like a mature person who would've never procrastinated this much in the first place.

"Have you taken the SAT yet?"

I nod, relieved to have this to say for myself: "Think I got, like, a thirty-one or something."

She sighs. "That's the ACT."

"I should get us another round," I say, picking up our empty shot cups. "What was your score?"

"Thirty-something."

ABRAM'S ACT SCORE is just a few lackadaisically smudged pencil marks away from my own. Safe bet he didn't force himself to take a month-long online prep course before test day, either.

Abram hands me my refill and then sits back down to explain. Turns out he was waiting to apply because he wasn't sure about committing to the tennis scholarship component, although he definitely wants to help out his mom with the tuition. This is a valid procrastination reason. The next one he gives, not so much.

"Plus, I wanted to see where you were going first." Him smiling like that, with his eyes downcast and hesitant to see my reaction, makes his admission seem extra cute. I pinch the bridge of my nose, reach down, and take my shot.

"You'd rather go your separate way?" he asks.

"Not necessarily. But I can't even commit to watching a movie with you, Abram—do you really want to be basing your first major life decision around my crazy whims?"

"Pretty much," he tells me. "Can't help it. Even before we started hanging out, I always hoped we'd end up at the same college, that things could maybe be different once we were away from everything. Like they are now. C'mon, let's matriculate somewhere together."

Could things really be the way they are now, all the time, if we attended the same university? Not as if I'd mind having Abram around. It's almost fun to picture him stopping by my dorm during one of the three times I'd allot him per day. He'd encourage me to leave my computer and go see what's on the menu at the dining hall. I'd act annoyed but eventually agree, not inviting my roommate to join us on our way out. The two of us would head off to the student center, avoiding eye contact with the students manning the activity booths in the lobby. Then one semester, when the inevitable happens and I lose my last marble, Abram could just drop me off at the mental institution on his way to the Love & Sexuality class I told him not to sign up for, save my cab driver the trip.

None of the above is ever going to happen. Ben Flynn could barely handle me leaving for four days; not realistic to think I could leave him for four years.

"I can't," I tell Abram. "My dad."

34

Juliette

"SAY THINGS WERE DIFFERENT with your dad," Abram says, sliding an envelope over to me, "would you consider going to this school?"

"Yes. Already applied there, pointlessly." I flick a tiny speck of Adderall off the stamp, left to wonder what might've been ingested. "But that doesn't mean it's the right college for you."

He smiles. "I trust your taste."

"Thanks, I'm still suspicious of it."

Abram opens the envelope and takes out the application, scanning it over for a minute. He gives me a thumbs-up, places it on the table, and asks me for a pen. I remove one from my purse, set it down on the application so the tip is pointing to the FIRST NAME field. My favorite Determined Abram look on his face, he puts his head down and goes to work. I allow myself a few minutes of feeling hopeful about the future.

ABRAM

THIS STARTED SUCKING shortly after I wrote my Social Security number in the second box. Helps to have my hopefully college-bound incentive right in front of me, checking on my progress every once in a while, in between staring at the laptop she somehow squeezed into her bottomless purse. When she thinks I'm far enough along, Juliette sweetens the pot by bringing up a hypothetical vacation with her and me this summer, preferably during the freshman orientation she's theoretically planning to skip. Maybe not the best idea to be anti before our first semester starts, but we'll see; it's not like she's never changed her mind before.

"What if we went to Russia?" she says, pulling up the streets of Moscow to the screen, via Google Earth. "Never mind. Something's off."

We start trying to come up with the best tourist-attracting slogan for Moscow, writing each down on the back of one of my envelopes.

She goes first: *Moscow, because you gotta kill yourself somewhere, right?!*

My first attempt: *Moscow, because we solemnly swear our Internet's not frozen anymore.*

Her turn: *Moscow, because your prostitute's waiting . . . don't forget your rubles, sexy!*

Me: *Moscow, because, wouldn't you know, the pits of hell are completely booked up this season.*

The last one has the unfortunate side effect of being

clever enough to make her think I can write my own essay, a task I was angling to get her help on.

"What about Paris?" she says, telling me she's always wanted to go, only not with our weird, just-one-of-the-students French teacher and a group of fundraising classmates. We take a virtual stroll along the Champs-Élysées until she accidentally lands us in a narrow alleyway—"A mugger's paradise" is how she describes the dingy ambiance, rather accurately. I take her hand in mine. "For safety purposes," I tell her. She smiles at the laptop, but it bounces back up to me, the intended recipient, from the screen.

"Excuse me . . . Angela?"

I glance up to see a short, overeager woman in her late twenties standing in front of the table we're using. Juliette's still looking down at Paris.

Juliette

I'M BEING CONVERSATIONALLY MUGGED, and there's nothing Abram or anyone else can do about it. My attacker is waving now . . . as if me ignoring her from two feet away is a big misunderstanding. If she says "Yoohoo!" or "Google Earth to Angie!" I'm throwing my coffee at her neck, fingers crossed it's still hot enough.

"Angela?"

Finally, I look up. Janette the barista is wearing her off-duty sweatpants and a knit cap (with tassels!) she's mistaking for quirky-cute. I shoot her an impatient look like the rude wannabe French tourist I am.

"Janette," she says in her American chipmunk voice, pointing to herself. "Remember me from the other day?"

"Yes, I think so. . . ." I say, leaving as much room for doubt as possible—too much and Janette will feel compelled to provide an eyewitness account of our transaction (*Are you sure? You were wearing the same black zip-up jacket with a similar pair of black . . .*). She glances over at Abram—looks back at me like, *So this is the guy!*—perhaps expecting me to introduce them. Then she realizes how long she'll be waiting for that.

"I don't mean to bother y'all during your coffee. I almost said something the other day, but I looked up and you were gone. You're a really fast walker."

There's a gleam in Abram's eye like, *Yep, that's my girl (problem).*

Janette points to my venti cup. "You look so similar to this nice woman who used to come in here and order that exact same drink," she continues. "She was so tiny but could drink enough coffee for someone twice her size. Actually, she's why I'm rocking the long-bob these days, although it didn't turn out quite the same as hers. . . ." She removes her cap so we can examine the hair failure underneath.

"Sorry, I don't know anyone with hair like that," I tell Janette, as if there *must* be some mistake.

35

Juliette

"HELLO, JANETTE," Abram says, extending his hand. "I'm Angela's travel-mate, Philip."

Travel-mate? I couldn't have talked around our status better myself. Really sweet he's taken the initiative to select a fake name and bring himself down to my level—much better than flowers. Wish I didn't have to hide my appreciation from Janette.

"So the name Sharon Flynn doesn't ring a bell?" she asks me.

The lie I'd prepared gets stuck mid-throat. I can't remember the last time anyone's said my mom's name around me—Dad stopped saying it long before she died—and it hasn't become easier to hear with the passage of time. The old me would power through the sinking feeling, cling to the Angela ruse like it's all I have left in the world, re-distance myself from my mom. The new me went skinny-dipping a few days ago and never washed back to shore.

"Sharon Flynn was my aunt," I confess, and it feels so freeing to be halfway honest.

Janette puts her hand on her chest like this is a huge shock she isn't responsible for giving herself. Then she launches into a poorly received Vagina Monologue about how Sharon was one of her favorite customers, and when my mom didn't show up whatever week she told Janette she'd be back to the island, Janette googled her name and found that horrible newspaper article.

"The picture of that car . . ." she says, shaking her head. "I'm so sorry you and your family had to see that."

My eyes narrow into blades. "It was nothing compared to seeing her in a casket."

Abram squirms in his chair, picking at the cuticles I already pushed back last night for him.

"Right . . . of course," Janette says apologetically. "I was sad for weeks, so I can't even imagine how y'all must've felt. It's just so unfair, you know? How quickly someone can be taken away like that? I really thought she was someone special."

"You did?" I say, dropping my guard for a second.

"Of course. She'd take the time to ask how my day was, get to know me a little bit . . . and, well, she always tipped."

My mom *was* a generous tipper. I'd forgotten that.

"Did she tell you anything more about herself?" I ask Janette.

"Just that she'd made some mistakes but she was happier than she'd ever been. She was going to start working less, spending more time with the people she most cared about."

I frown. She lost me.

"She seemed like she had a plan, you know?" Janette adds.

I nod. With her again.

"Anything about her daughter?" I ask, and my pulse quickens. Too much coffee . . . Janette . . . Mom. Abram takes my hand into his.

Janette smiles. "She showed me her daughter's picture once. She seemed very proud."

I close my eyes, waiting for Janette to add, *And yet distracted by her phone at the same time,* or accuse me of identity fraud because she's seen my picture. Which means my mom had one stored in her phone, easily accessible. Why hadn't I noticed? I certainly went through her texts enough at the hospital.

I reopen my eyes. Janette remains silent. Miraculously, she's run out of things to say.

I stand up and start grabbing anything that looks remotely like mine, trying to head off any further embarrassment. Abram slides my purse from my shoulder and places it over his like it's the latest in man-bag styles for well-traveled guys named Philip, says a hurried good-bye on our behalf, and leads me toward the door. As we're walking out, I stop, turn around, and mouth a *Thank you* to Janette, who's now at the counter ordering a drink. She smiles sadly, like she wishes there was more she could do. There's not. There's just nothing.

ABRAM

DOES IT GO WITHOUT SAYING that I'm here if she wants to talk about what just happened? Because maybe that's why she hasn't responded to anything I've said since we left Starbucks. In the meantime, I'll keep working on my one-way communication.

"Does Angela have any interest in napping with Philip when they arrive home?" I ask.

"None whatsoever," Juliette says, but at least she replied. A minute later, she takes my hand. Relieved I haven't lost her, I kiss the top of her head and tell her I'm proud of her for confronting whatever that was. She laughs, doesn't recognize the progress she's making.

Nearing the house, we see a man and a woman, dressed in expensive-looking tennis whites, peering into the window and probably wondering what's going on in the living room. I think Juliette's had as many unsolicited conversations as she can handle today.

"Want to run in the opposite direction?" I whisper.

"Yes, please," she says, even though we've just been spotted. Terry and Linda McEvans are waving at us like they can't believe how perfect their timing is.

36

ABRAM

"DON'CH'ALL JUST HATE nosy neighbors?" Terry says.

"No way," I reply, "nosy neighbors are awesome."

Juliette nods in sarcastic agreement.

Terry laughs and wipes a smudge of green clay from his calf before initiating our man-hug ritual. The girls are groaning at how lame it is—Juliette actually says, "Lame"—so we repeat the steps in slow motion.

"My husband specializes in asking people questions they can't answer honestly," Linda says, flashing Juliette a wide smile from underneath her visor. Everything about Linda's outfit matches, right down to the thin pink stripes around the edge of her socks. "He should've been a politician."

"Maybe in our next life together, my first lady. In the meantime, I'm hoping this small contingent of good-looking young people will vote yes to dining out with us old folks tonight?"

Juliette and I look at each other and laugh in uncomfortable unison.

"Is that a yes and a yes I see on your faces?" Terry squints and places his hand to his forehead as a shield. "My vision ain't what it used to be."

"Normally you could count us in," I lie, "but Juliette was actually planning on making me dinner tonight."

"Aw, that's so sweet," Linda says, eyes twinkling.

"Is it?" Juliette says, scrunching up her nose.

I pat my stomach like I've been looking forward to her cooking up some 1950s romance on my behalf.

"Don't feel bad about us having to invite Diabetic Bob and Arthritic Nancy," Terry says with mock sadness. "We love hearing about how much better Nancy's circulation is down south."

"Riveting," Linda concurs.

"We'll go to dinner with you," Juliette says.

Linda recovers quickest from the shock. "Great! The menu is just okay," she says, "but Terry likes to go there for the corny seafood ambiance."

Terry clears his throat. "Don't forget karaoke Saturdays, dear."

"We'll leave before it starts," Linda promises us.

"No, no, let's go during prime time," Juliette says agreeably, in an enthusiastic voice I don't recognize. "Abram loves singing almost as much as I love cooking."

"I do?"

"You do," Juliette confirms. "Remember that one time I was really upset about something unimportant, and you turned to me and just started singing a Jack Johnson song, in perfect pitch?"

This never happened, but Linda thinks the prospect of it is really sweet, too, for some reason.

Juliette

ABRAM'S WORRYING about me again. Barely left my side since we walked into the house. Now he's sitting on the toilet, lid closed, while I finish getting ready for dinner with the McEvans twins, whom I refuse to hide from. Otherwise, I'll just end up confining myself to a controlled environment where nothing changes (or else!), like my father's office, for depressing example.

Back to Abram. He's wearing a faded, fitted T-shirt over the top of a long-sleeve T-shirt, paired with the white linen shorts I bought him at the tourist trap down the road.

"I think the first layer of T-shirt gives the outfit a dressier quality, don't you?" he asks, catching my eye before several strands of damp hair fall into his. He blows them back, smiles at me when they don't stay in place.

"Now that you mention it . . . not really," I say, turning around to cut a string from one of his sleeves. "It works for you, though."

"You look really good tonight," he says. "Beautiful."

"Thanks." I turn back around and frown into the bathroom mirror, examining what's gone wrong with my face since a few seconds ago. Good thing I'll be attending college virtually. University of Phoenix Online, here I come! The anticipation is making me want to pluck something. I take a deep breath and try to focus on something positive, like Abram, instead. "Your facial stubble looks especially attractive tonight. And your tan."

I'm sure it'll look really good onstage when he's filling the restaurant with his song.

I ask him to hold still for a second, acting concerned about seeing a foreign object in his eye. Then I reveal the tweezers and start plucking a few stray hairs between his eyebrows. He knows it's what I really wanted to do all along, barely winces when I tug.

"I shouldn't have signed you up for karaoke," I say. "I'll get you out of it."

He shrugs. "The mood for a serenade might strike me."

"I'll throw a fork at it if I see it getting close."

He laughs before his blue eyes turn serious. "You sure you're okay being around Linda?"

"I'm sick of hiding from people," I say, even though we both know I'm not quite there yet.

Abram suggests we create a safe word, just in case one of us wants to leave before the other. I like how he's pretending the flight risk in that scenario could turn out to be him. And I *love* his idea, more excited about it than the dinner itself. I drop the tweezers onto the bathroom countertop with a clang, and we head outside to wait for Linda and Terry to pick us up, going back and forth rejecting each other's safe-word choices—his worst being "diarrhea," mine being "lady-cramps"—until we settle on "Moscow."

If nothing else, we'll always have Moscow, sort of.

37

Juliette

THE MCEVANSES BUZZ UP to the driveway in their gleaming golf cart. It might be nicer than Heidi's car, Vulva the Volvo. Ha, Heidi. If girlfriend were here to embarrass me (from a place of love) right now, she'd sneak a glance at Terry's salt-and-pepper mouth whiskers before asking if I'm excited about my mustache ride. In conclusion, I'm with the right person tonight: Abram.

As he and I hop into the back seat, Terry says something about how we "clean up real nice." Must be hard to see my all-black, funereal ensemble, but Abram does look rather dashingly laid-back. Terry and Linda are dressed to the nines in a sea of khaki and island-friendly pinks and blues. Linda greets us warmly and apologizes to me for any future hair problems the golf cart's windscreen doesn't prevent. I point to one of my stray frizzlets like there's already a problem in progress, and she does an admirable job of sounding empathetic despite her newscaster coif looking primed and ready for tonight's top story. Meanwhile, Terry pretends he can't find the golf-cart path at first, driving along the sidewalk instead—one of his better attempts at humor—and then we ride off into the sunset, toward the restaurant.

"Terry, this golf cart runs so smoothly," I say, winking at Abram. I bet him ten dollars of our parents' money I could make Terry say something about his golf cart "purring like a kitten."

"Why, thank you," Terry says, "just got 'er tuned up last week."

So close.

"Does she have a name?" Abram asks, trying to throw him off.

"Barbaraaaaa Aaaaann," Terry sings in Beach Boy falsetto. I ask what kind of motor Barbara Ann runs on, noting how I can barely hear her. Terry gives us the make and model before adding, "She sure purrs like a kitten, does she not, or does she not?"

I flash Abram a winning smile as Linda tells Terry he sure isn't allowed to use that phrase anymore. Ugh, I really do like her. I ask where she found the huge purse she's carrying as the boys discuss how often they get their rackets restrung. Everyone else is smiling, relaxed, and I feel even more like the grandma of the group—pretending to take it all in but biding my time until I can change back into my comfortable clothes.

The restaurant is in line with the low expectations Linda set for it earlier: signage with crab-catching jokes, plastic fish entangled in faux netting, canoe paddles insisting the term "cabrewing" is clever, and so on. I do appreciate the darkness of the ambiance, how I can barely see the faces of our fellow diners.

Terry points out that the karaoke stage is in the back room and pats Abram on the shoulder, winking at me. It's one of the only winks from an older man I've gotten that hasn't made me want to exfoliate (Abram winking when he's using his creepy grandpa voice doesn't count). Linda chats with the maître d' for a second before he tips his captain's hat and escorts us to his "best table on the Poop Deck." I'm assuming it's a poop joke Terry's whispering into Abram's ear on the way.

The Poop Deck is outside on the covered patio, and our table really might be their best. I can hear the tide washing in.

"Hmm, I'm not sure who to give the Best-Looking Couple Award to tonight," the maître d' says, handing us each a menu. Terry replies that he'll take the award along with the check at the end of the meal; Abram and I are completely fine with both claims.

When the maître d' leaves, Terry inhabits the role of bartender and asks what we'd like to drink, laughing when we both answer water. "I meant alcoholic beverages." Linda looks concerned but backs off when Terry says, "I think Abram and Juliette deserve a drink if they'd like one, don't you, dear?" She ends up ordering two vodka cranberries; Terry two Jack & Sevens. The waiter doesn't blink, just brings the cocktails a minute later. Thankfully, no one gives a toast.

ABRAM

I THOUGHT ABOUT GIVING A TOAST but couldn't think of what to say. *Cheers, to the dynamic not being as awkward as originally anticipated!* In conclusion, weird things tempt me sometimes. *Cheers, to weird temptations!*

The food arrives fast, mostly in silver buckets. The second round of drinks arrives even quicker. Terry keeps looking over at the karaoke room to see if they're starting soon. Eventually, he gets up and brings back a thick song catalog. He suggests a game of karaoke roulette—boys against girls—whereby we each choose a song for our competitors to perform and they have to sing it no matter what. I anticipate this being the first game Juliette refuses to play this vacation, but she's kept quiet so far, just listening to Linda complain about Terry giving her "Somewhere Over the Rainbow" last week.

"The crowd just sat there and died," Linda says, "while I thought about how I was going to kill Terry." Then she puts her hand to her diamond starfish necklace and apologizes profusely.

Juliette explains there's no need to apologize or avoid hypothetically killing people on our account. "I do it all the time," she assures Linda. "Now let's watch these boys commit musical suicide, shall we?"

Juliette

LINDA AND I are huddled together over the song catalog. She's searching for a tune that would require the guys to sing almost their entire song in falsetto, keeps picking out hits by the Bee Gees as I shake my head.

"What about this one?" I say, pointing to "You've Lost That Lovin' Feelin'," hoping maybe I'll glean some tips from the lyrics.

"I am *such* a sucker for that song," Linda whispers intensely. "Plus, Terry will sound terrible singing it." Then she cackles, and, yes, it didn't take her long to get wasted. One more drink and maybe she'll forget we're slated to perform, too. Scary, why am I putting myself *so far* out there again? I filled out the sign-up sheet with fake names a little while ago, but the DJ was giving me a suspicious look (I've never been less offended), so Angela Buckley's no-show performance of "Love Shack" isn't likely to delay the inevitable much longer.

A few minutes later, Abram and Terry get called up to the stage. They're already right there in front of it, hunting through the prop box that sits atop one of the speakers. Terry selects the Steve Martin–inspired cap-with-arrow-sticking-through-it, which doesn't get any funnier when he slaps it on his head. Abram looks over at me and points to his stuffed-frog hat like, *This okay?* I smile supportively and give him a thumbs-down.

The music starts. As soon as the boys begin dancing, bending their knees to the rhythm, I'm laughing. Abram takes on the first part of the Righteous Brother with the lower register, blowing a kiss toward me when he sings the "kiss your lips" line. And then Terry really goes for the gusto, in a musical styling that's more spoken-word staccato than singing, reaching out to Linda when he belts "your fingertips." Abram has that roadkill-in-headlights look on his face where he's realizing his partner sucks and he wasn't really prepared to carry the entire performance load on his own shoulders. Linda's about to feel the same way. They make it through with a lot of help from the forgiving crowd, and when Abram bounds off the stage toward me, I can't stop myself from kissing him. Just a peck, but it's enough to draw a few whistles from Terry the One-Man Peanut Gallery that I barely notice.

"Angela Buckley going once, going twice . . . okay, I need Juliette and Linda up to the stage, please," the DJ says in a voice that's trying to be more excited than it really is. "Juliette and Lindaaaaaaa."

Linda takes my hand in a defiant display of girl power, reminding me to hold my head high and pretend whatever happens is intentional. We go forth into the fog billowing up from the smoke machine, the boys hooting and hollering about what's in store for the room.

I wrap my hand around the smooth throat of my mic stand like I'm about to strangle it. Linda walks behind hers and starts adjusting it like she's <insert dark-haired songstress in her age demographic>. Linda Ronstadt? She could be the real Linda Ronstadt for all I know.

The music starts and the prompter reveals what the boys have chosen for us: "Single Ladies (Put a Ring on It)." Um, that isn't even a duet. Linda was right; we should've falsetto'd them over with the Bee Gees.

Linda has an in-tune voice with an abundance of vibrato

that makes the line "up in da club" sound like it was borrowed from a religious education song. At least her shoes are cute. Mine? Louboutins, thanks for asking. Got them from the Salvation Army, of all places.

My turn. I'm singing. It's weird. If I had to describe my voice in two words, I'd go with "mousegirl rasp." Not "Kelly Clarkson," which is what Linda compares it to during the instrumental break. I'm having too much fun to make fun of myself.

ABRAM

PEOPLE MIGHT NOT CHANGE very often, but they can still surprise you. Almost every rough edge in Juliette's voice gets filed down when she's singing. There's a soul to her tone and nary a note goes flying off where it shouldn't. She even manages to make Linda's contributions sound like they're supposed to be there.

"My wife has a lot of gifts," Terry says, "but the gift of music ain't one of 'em."

The girls rush off the stage, and I'm so proud of Juliette I have to kiss her several times. I tell her how amazing she is, because she is, and that she should consider trying out for a reality show. She laughs it off, saying it'd be way too easy for the producers to give her the crazy-girl edit. I kiss her again, her options still very much open in my book, except when it comes to me. Not fair that anything would ever try to pass itself off as more important than us and this, but that's life, I guess—a bunch of crap competing for your attention when the best things are right in front of your face.

"Get a timeshare, you two!" Terry calls out from the sidelines, but he says it after we're finished having our own-little-world moment.

38

Juliette

BACK AT OUR TABLE, Terry just gave the Best Performance Award to Abram and himself. Linda's arguing about it, and I'm confused by why she's chosen this exact moment to start taking him seriously. If it makes her feel any better, she's a shoo-in for the Drunkest Person Award.

"Gulls' room?" I ask Linda, and Abram's impressed by my using the restaurant's bathroom terminology. She nods, shooting her Buoy, Terry, one last glare. He acts like he's scared, but not really, and her cheeks turn Scarlett O'Hara with fury again. She starts heading in the direction opposite the bathrooms, almost falls headfirst over the Poop Deck, so I hold her hand and guide her the rest of the way. She should definitely take one of the silver food buckets home and place it next to her bedside.

"Jesus God, I really have to pee," she tells me with a desperate look on her face. I hold the door for her. Inside, Linda can't decide if she can stomach the idea of doing her lady biz in a public stall, so she tries to distract herself by fixing her makeup. Seconds later, she's sprinting for the toilet. Deep down, we're all four years old. She begins the process of taking forever, during which I enjoy the rest of my karaoke adrenaline rush and look forward to holding Abram's strangely magnetic hand underneath the table upon our return. I'm staring at myself in the mirror when Linda emerges, feeling dirty about herself. She washes her hands several times before removing a tube of lipstick from her purse.

"Juliette, I owe you an apology," she says, as I hand her a blotting tissue.

"Not even, you hit some incredible notes out there."

"You're sweet, but I mean for the other day. I got to talking about Suzy and your parents and your loss—and the whole thing was so me-me-me—I hope I didn't make you feel bad."

I can't convince Linda there's no need to be sorry, so it's easier to just accept her third apology, which is also made straight from the bottom of her heart-shaped face. Every time I think we're heading back, she starts talking again.

"I just can't get over that y'all, you and Abram, are . . . together."

"Yes, it's pretty messed-up."

"No, it's greaaaat. It's so great. For crying out loud, you know where Terry and I met? In the bathroom of a Piggly Wiggly. I was debating whether to use their facilities when he barged in saying the 'men's shitter is out of service.' His exact words, of course."

Of course.

Linda hesitates, muttering something about Terry being mad at her for saying this, then brings it up anyway. "It's crazy how your mother . . . she just knew Abram was the right guy."

I blink once, twice, confused. "You mean *Ian*?"

"No, Abram," Linda says, smiling. "Sharon told me she thought he'd be perfect for you."

ABRAM

"JULIETTE JUST STEPPED OUT to get some air," Linda says, sitting down.

"Honey, it's raining," Terry points out.

"Well, yes, but she said she'd stand underneath the awning. I'm afraid I might've talked her ear off back there."

Terry shoots me a look like he knows how painful that is. Linda throws a small piece of cheese-biscuit at his face; he tries to catch it with his mouth, almost does. A minute or two later, I call Juliette's cell. It rings a million times, which is how I know something's not right. She usually sends her calls straight to voice mail.

"I shouldn't have brought up her mom," Linda says. "I thought she might want to . . . never mind, I should go check on her."

"That's okay." I stand up. "Please don't take this personally, but I'm ninety-nine percent sure she's already gone."

Terry insists I take his golf-cart keys, in case I can't find Juliette outside. "Lady Chatterley here and I were planning on closin' down this joint, anyway," he says, putting his arm around Linda. I thank the two of them for dinner and rush outside, find the golf cart parked beside a BMW like a regular car. The rain pounds onto the canvas roof above me. And Juliette's out there somewhere, without me to hold the umbrella for her, alone with her darkest thoughts.

39

ABRAM

COULDN'T FIND HER walking on the path or along the road back to the house. I burst through the front door, hair wet and matted to my forehead, wiping my feet on the entryway rug. I call out for her again and again, and the scene I'm creating feels too melodramatic in this moment. I hope it looks even more ridiculous in hindsight.

The kitchen is empty, quiet but for the consistent humming of the fridge she too-rarely opens and the squishing of my waterlogged flip-flops on the marble tile. I jog toward the living room, find our couch bed unmade, the way we left it after our wide-awake nap this afternoon. I slide open the door and step out onto the back deck. I look over toward the hot tub, wishing she were here to warn me away from it.

Juliette

FYI, I'LL NEVER BE in the hot tub.

Send.

ABRAM

SHE'S TEXTING! Although she hasn't responded to my follow-up question about her current location. Maybe because there's only one other place she could be.

Back in the house, I creak up the stairs wondering what could've drawn her to the second floor. An odd, ghostlike noise? No, if I had to guess, I'd say she's trying to prove something to herself. Or her mom.

Looking down the hallway to the master bedroom, I'm positive I closed the door on our way out a few days ago. In fact, Juliette asked me to both double-check and put a large object in front of it. The ottoman has been pushed to the side. The door is slightly ajar, a tiny stream of light poking through the crack.

Juliette

NO IDEA WHAT I'M TRYING to prove right now. That I'm crazy? That I wasn't just saying it all along? That I'm brave enough to be in the same room with my mom's alleged ghost, who probably isn't even interested, lying on the same bed where she fucked the father of the guy she thought was *perfect for me?*

You don't need to prove who you really are. You just are, comes the voice of my *Silence Speaks* audiobook narrator, a gentle reminder of why I stopped listening after chapter 4. He has a point, of course. This isn't me. It's a story I'm creating in my head right now, about a girl named Juliette overreacting to some surprising news about my mother's never-revealed knack for teen matchmaking, and the fact that her questions to me about Abram weren't being asked entirely for selfish reasons. The plot has nothing to do with who I am as a crazy person; it just seems that way because it's at the top of my mind trying to pass itself off as the most disturbing thing of all time.

What-ev-er, I hope Abram doesn't object to my slipping into something more comfortable. I slipped into something a lot less comfortable first—nothing but my bra and underwear—but then my mind was like, *Girl, who are you kidding? You should change.* So I listened to it. Always do.

ABRAM

I EASE OPEN THE DOOR and find her on the bed, waiting for me. Either me or a blizzard, because she's wearing my hoodie with her fleece over it, the hood drawn up over her head, her favorite gray scarf wrapped around her neck. Her legs, in contrast, are completely bare—free of all clothing from her cute little feet up to the tops of her thighs, where the mysterious fabric of her nude-colored panties begins. Pretty sure Juliette hates the word "panties." Her eyes are open; she's not moving. She looks so tired, frozen from the waist down, and much farther away from me than she really is.

40

Juliette

A REVELATION HIT ME as I was lying here a few minutes ago, staring down at my wheezing bosom, waiting for Abram to swing through the door (like he is now) and take advantage of me—my body is still unappealing! And cold. So I put a few layers on and compromised. Ta-da, now I'm like an outdoorsy lesbian up top, and a reluctant whore with mother issues on the bottom. Let's call the whole thing off.

Too late, Abram's shutting the door behind him. While he's removing his flip-flops, I bite my lips in a futile attempt to make them look bee-stung (by the same bee who does Angelina Jolie's). He looks over my way again, feasts his eyes on me and all my phony wanton, the very antithesis of come-hitherishness.

"You okay?" he asks.

"Why do you ask?" I say, like nothing's out of the ordinary, and motion for him to join me. He walks over and sits down on my side of the bed. He's damp but not as drenched as I thought. I have a daydream about Terry handing Abram the keys to Barbara Ann with a can't-live-with-'em look on his face, and I want to ask if I'm right, but I also don't want to make Abram feel weird about having a bonding moment with an older, slightly annoying male father-figure.

"Your hair isn't wet," Abram says, smoothing a humidity frizzlet back from my forehead.

"Cab."

He smiles halfway before his face turns serious again. "What happened?"

"Linda told me my mom thought you and I would be perfect together."

"Okay." Abram pauses for a moment, thinks about this carefully, runs his fingers through his own hair. "That's not such a bad thing, is it?"

I look around for a mask to wear so I don't hurt his feelings.

ABRAM

"FRUSTRATING," JULIETTE SAYS, from behind a throw pillow. "How could she be so *right* about something she had no clue about?"

"You think she's right?" I say, and she can probably hear the smile in my voice, because she throws the pillow at me.

"Don't change the subject."

I scan my mind again for something else to make her feel better, end up landing on someone else. My mom.

"This probably isn't relevant, but want to know what my mom always says about stuff like this?"

"Not really."

"She says, 'Abram, moms just know.' "

"Know what?"

"Everything."

"There's not more to it than that?" Juliette asks.

I shake my head. "She can't really explain how she picks up on things. Maybe your mom had that kind of inexplicable intuition, too? Even if she never completely earned it."

Juliette looks highly skeptical but slightly less miserable. I take both of her hands into mine. "Can I do anything to bring you back from the past?"

"Yes," she says, "start taking advantage of me right now."

Juliette

ABRAM HASN'T BEGUN ravaging my supple body yet, so I sit up and start peeling his dual shirts from his stomach. The process is less complicated than I'm making it seem. He has to assist once I've rolled them up to his neck. I throw the wad of clothing off to the side, knocking the lamp off the nightstand. Somehow, it doesn't break. I look down and see his shorts bunching up against his belt buckle, unable to determine if I got the wrong size or if it's *that.* Probably not ready to deal with it if I can't even refer to it by name.

"I don't have a condom," Abram says.

"I'm on the pill."

He seems surprised.

"For psychotic hormone regulation, not because I'm a whore."

The passion in the air curls up and dies in front of me. I reignite it by reaching toward his belt buckle, working my fingers inside the leather loop, pulling, unhinging, freeing the strap and unbuttoning the top of his shorts. His stomach isn't nearly as tan in this region, so I guess this is the skin I should've been competing against all along. Perfect, my left leg is going numb. On a scale of 1–10, this sex we're about to embark upon is going to be the dash in between the numbers. Off the charts, all my fault. Abram will try to steal all the blame, the only thing he's selfish about taking. I really just want to make him feel better in a non-fake, preferably non-verbal way that doesn't lead to a mess. I want him to feel . . . nothing. Except me. And my thoughts on all subjects, which are usually the correct ones, except during times like these, when they're ganging up on me and I need his help.

ABRAM

THIS IS ONE OF THOSE ideas that's going to start out being hers, but end up looking like mine. Because I should know better? I don't think anyone would believe that. Because I'm the guy? Dude, that's more like it.

Too many outside influences. Between the Janette encounter, the girl talk with Linda, the Adderall she probably took afterward to make herself feel back in control of the situation, and the creepy master-bedroom setting she's using to unnecessarily torture herself, it's too much about everything else, not enough about us.

That being said, for the first time in my life I can understand how my dad could lose his mind over a girl . . . over and over again. I don't really want to relate to him in this particular way, especially in his bed, but I'm not sure I'll be able to deny it. Doesn't seem like as much of a choice when you've already started making the mistake. Nor does it help when your shorts are unzipped like mine are now.

41

ABRAM

JULIETTE'S LEFT LEG is no longer cooperating, and neither of us seems eager to climb into these particular bedsheets, so I'm able to convince her to go back downstairs to the moderate discomfort of our couch bed. When we reach the living room, she asks me to take off my shorts before joining her. I comply. And then we're all the way underneath the covers, heads included.

"Okay," Juliette whispers, "ready as I'll ever be." She shuts her eyes. "I mean, when you are."

Juliette

I SQUEEZE MY LIDS TOGETHER as tightly as possible, the crow's feet pecking away at my skin, preparing for *the worst*. And then I feel Abram's lashes on my cheek. Um, aren't these called butterfly kisses? Primarily given after bedtime prayer? Per the song that a creepy dad wrote for his little girl while putting little white flowers all up in her hair? I open my eyes, prepared to mention this to Abram, but he's already humming the song. Our laughter breaks the tension just enough for reality—banished until now, thanks to me—to set in. And then he kisses me, draws me into his lips, brings back that warm, Abramy, heart-blanketing feeling I can't push aside anymore.

"Did the Asian take your virginity?" I ask, unable to stop myself from killing the mood one last time. He removes his lips from the spot on my neck that makes me crazy (among other things), looking up at me like I'm about to kill him, too.

ABRAM

"DID SHE?" Juliette demands.

"Almost. Long story . . ."

"When has that ever stopped you?"

I tell her it happened a month after the accident, in the movie-screening room of the Asian girl's basement, and it felt way too soon to be getting any action. Juliette's not mad; she's excited: "I knew there was a reason I hated her." Then she laughs about how the Asian thought she could make my grief go away with some after-school ass, and I'm thinking, *Perhaps, but she's also kind of a sex freak. An accomplished one with great homework scores who knows what she wants (penis, Carnegie Hall).* Time to change the subject.

"What about you?" I ask.

"You wouldn't know him."

She explains that he's in college now, getting his B.A. in Nobody Cares. A few seconds later, she admits he doesn't exist. Can't say I'm disappointed this particular part of her sexual history is fictional, right before we change our stories for real. First, I need to tell her something that I don't want lumped in with the physical side of things.

"Did you know . . . that . . . I love you?"

She looks at me curiously, wondering what I'm *really* trying to say. The "I love you" component was pretty much the gist, but I should've just said it outright, let it sink or swim on its own, without testing the waters first.

"I love you, Juliette. There's nothing about you—no secret, no pill, no past relationship—that could make me stop trying to love you more every day. You don't have to say it ba—"

"I love you, too." She places her hand on my stomach, rests it there. "I didn't recognize it at first . . . probably because it's the truth . . . but I'm pretty sure I've loved you for a long time."

"Like, CVS-at-first-sight long time?"

"Longer," she says, grimacing. "Since back when we were whales."

I squeeze her hand. "How could I forget?"

After that, we deduce that we've probably had sexual relations as whales already, so there's no need to rush into anything as humans until we're fully prepared to rush into it. Two seconds later, I think I'm ready.

42

Juliette

LYING HERE IN OUR COUCH BED, running my fingers through Abram's wavy-thick hair and picking the occasional fuzz ball from it, is so much more relaxing than the irresponsible intercourse I'd hastily planned for us. I almost fell asleep a few minutes ago until a spider began *crawling up my thigh* . . . a pulse-pounder that turned out to be Abram's leg hair performing its late-night tarantula impersonation.

"How can I help you relax?" he says groggily, turning over to face me.

"Not possible," I say. "But you could try telling me a story if it makes you feel better."

He furrows his brow, actually considering the request. "Genre?"

"Romance," I answer. "Not too much love, though. And with us as the main characters, but me as a less-depressing version of myself. Or just do your own thing, sorry."

"There once was a whale from Nantucket," he begins. "She

was a female whale named Angela Buckley who frowned her fair share. She was also pretty skinny by her species' standards, although her absence of blubber didn't take much, if anything, away from her sleek, intimidating beauty. It just made her cold all the time."

He kisses me softly on my forehead, asks what I think so far. I curl up against his chest, molding my entire body into his, letting him know he has my interest. "Smart to abandon the 'ucket' rhyming scheme early on," I say quietly. "Angela the whale sounds like a crazy B."

"Funny you should mention Angela's mental state," Abram says. "She wanted her fellow whales to misread her as inaccessible, yes, and believe she had no interest in getting to know them. Not because Angela thought her whale poo didn't stink—she just had a lot of rules and walls and self-restraining orders on top of being sad, scared, admittedly overmedicated, and, most of all, lost. But then, one day, she found a strapping male whale named Philip with the healthiest appetite she'd ever seen, filling up his convenience basket with food at her favorite twenty-four-hour whale pharmacy."

He pauses so we can brainstorm a good name for a whale pharmacy. His entries: Rite Whale, Whale Pharm, Whalegreens. Mine: SeaVS, Pills & Krill . . . and then I forfeit because I swear on the Little Mermaid's humanity I was going to say Whalegreens.

"Great, so Angela and Philip were both at Whalegreens," Abram continues. "Philip the whale, who was a bit sad and lonely himself at the time, was waiting for the prescription that had contributed to his excessive sleeping and eating of great-tasting junk such as Reese's Peanut Butter Cups and pizza-on-a-bagel, but I digress."

He digresses straight into the kitchen, microwaves our snack, and returns with a plate of pepperoni bagel bites. We eat and Abram tells the rest of his story, our story, in a way that makes me realize how in love we really are without making me uncomfortable. When I ask him if there will be anything close to a decent ending for Angela and Philip, he says it doesn't matter, because *at this very moment*, they're together, happy.

43

Juliette

"READY?" ABRAM ASKS ME, as we're packing up the car Monday morning.

I give him the facial expression his question deserves.

"Me neither."

I hate endings, especially after enjoying what happened beforehand. But it's time to leave. I'll miss you, non-barking dogs at the beach. Thanks for the memories, couch bed. You weren't as creepy as I made you out to be, house. Each good-bye is like a death. And we all know how healthily I deal with that fact of life.

Nevertheless, I'd like to think I've changed a bit for the better these past few days. That I won't regress to taking too many pills, being a reliable no-show to parties, going about my business like it's just another day at the office inside my head. Crazy, Inc. has a one-man Human Resources Department now, in the form of Abram, who reminds me everything is going to be fine whether I ignore it or not. Yes, Abram made our last mandatory run on the beach enjoyable, our last conversation with Linda and Terry manageable, our last kiss on the couch bed worth getting the bed back out for because we almost forgot to have one last kiss on the couch bed.

Together, we pull out of the driveway and onto the road.

"Squirrel chunks," I say, pointing toward the curb.

Abram smiles. "Or . . . a brown golf towel."

"Jesus."

"Your driving is looking really accurate, though."

"Thanks," I say, re-gripping the wheel. "You're up, one-to-zero."

If we ever become the kind of couple who tell people we're a couple, I'm pretty sure we won't bring out the worst in each other, on purpose. That's not really something to brag about, I'm just saying . . . we make a good couple.

ABRAM

I'M PROUD OF JULIETTE for taking the first leg of the trip. Even if it's a short leg. When she reaches the stop sign just past the security gate, we get out of the car and trade places. I manage to kiss her in passing before getting back into the car. Twenty minutes later, as I'm rolling up beside the tollbooth, she leans over and kisses me. Against all whatnot, we're definitely in love. I hope she's still feeling it after I make this announcement.

"I sent you an e-mail this morning."

After recovering from the shock, she checks her phone. "Why is there a spreadsheet labeled 'Subtracterall' attached to it?"

"Open it up and find out."

She does her nose-scrunch thing. "I'll save it for later."

"There are some excellent formulas inside, trust me."

Juliette downloads the file and starts reviewing the recovery plan I've laid out for her, which includes dates, dosages, and even a Strategies column that I've pretty much memorized.

1. Take a deep breath and text Abram. (He likes phone calls, too, but knows you're not a fan.)
2. Let yourself laugh at the humorous Emoji he texts back along with another open invitation to his basement.
3. Go to Abram's basement and/or let Abram pick you up and eventually take you underground.
4. Share a guilt-free snack with Abram.
5. Kiss him often (this really helps).
6. If, after all that, you still want to pop a pill, Abram and the dog will not judge you.
7. Don't give yourself a hard time if you slip up along the way. Fail better next time. With Abram.

"So, whataya say?"

She nods and agrees to try it. That's all anyone could ever ask, including me.

"You know I'm your girlfriend when we get back home, right?" she says, handing me a coconut water.

"Never considered you anything else."

44

Juliette

THIS CAN'T BE MY HOUSE. The freak haven Abram just pulled up in front of is far too welcoming, like a place where children can giggle and play nearby without fear or parental guardians. Strands of white lights have been strung diagonally along the columns by the front door, perfectly spaced. Matching pots of poinsettias sit beside them. Three cranberry-infested wreaths hang above each garage, the doors of which have been left open for our neighbors to just walk right up and annoy us. Dad's car is parked in his spot, but that doesn't stop me from calling his cell for an explanation. He's not answering. Abram doesn't think it's time to alarm the police just yet. He offers to accompany me inside, and I try to entertain the possibility of Abram and my father in the same room together. It only works if I don't have to be there, too.

"Just to make sure everything's okay," he tells me, "then I'll leave immediately."

"I bet you say that to all your paranoid girlfriends."

"Is it working?"

"Yes, actually. Remind me to have you check the closets for intruders."

He gets my suitcase out of the trunk and rolls it into the garage beside me. The door is unlocked, WTF. Abram points up . . . to the mistletoe hanging above our heads. Nightmare. I kiss him back, anyway.

The temperature inside the house is warm, almost as if we're encouraging our guests to kick off their shoes and stay awhile.

"Want me to take off my flip-flops?" Abram asks.

"That's okay."

We step into the kitchen. "Dad!" I call out. He never answers—prefers to draw me into his office so he doesn't have to move—just thought I'd try for the millionth time.

I'm about to offer Abram the nothing we have to eat or drink, but then I think twice and open the fridge. The shelves have been stocked with soda, sliced watermelon, grapes that have already been picked from their stems and placed in a plastic container, meats and cheeses that would've required talking to the person manning the deli counter.

We find my father's office recently cleaned, not a stack of coffee-stained papers in sight. The dimmer switch has been slid up to its Medium setting, not its usual Completely Off. A candle sits flickering on his desk, its pine-tree scent filling the room with the nauseating stench of Christmas spirit.

Dad's chair has been swiveled away from the door. He's there. Typing away at his keyboard, in another world, writing.

Some things never change . . . until they have to, because I really want to go to college with Abram.

ABRAM

JULIETTE WALKS OVER and starts inspecting her father, pretends to be weirded out by him wearing jeans and a polo instead of sweatpants and a flannel, but my hunch is she's relieved by the transformation. Then she smiles and hugs her dad, and they stay like that for a minute, giving me a chance to process that I'm really a fly on the wall in her house.

Juliette steps back and introduces us in her impatient way: "Dad, Abram. Abram, blahhh, I hate introductions."

Ben Flynn doesn't smile at me, just stands up and wraps my hand in his cold palm. "Thank you, young man," he says as we shake. I must look confused by the somber display of gratitude, because he adds, "For keeping my daughter company these past few months."

It's like getting extra credit for homework I would've done anyway, but I take it and tell him it was no big deal.

"Except it was, because I'm high-maintenance," Juliette says, guiding me to the couch so I can have a seat. Ben Flynn sits, as well. She remains standing. "Not to change the subject, Father, but haven't we always been vaguely annoyed by Christmas?"

"We have been, yes," Ben Flynn admits. "I suppose I thought it wouldn't hurt to give Christmas another try. Plus, I got you a gift."

"Thanks, but please no." She thinks this over again. "What is it?"

"We have to pick it up together, but see how much fun we're having with the holidays already?" Ben Flynn says, rubbing his hands together facetiously. "What do you think of the lights, Abram?"

I look up at Juliette, then over to her dad. "I like them. Left me wanting more."

She sighs, sits down next to me as I ask her dad what his latest book is about. "It's about a man and a woman who meet at CVS," he explains, and Juliette doesn't look surprised. Her idea, I gather. The rest of his synopsis sounds familiar, but not *too* familiar in a way that would make me think Ben Flynn just got back from hiding out in the closet of the same beach house as us.

"Do you have a title yet?" I ask.

"I've grown partial to Juliette's suggestion of a few weeks ago: *Prescription for Love.*"

"That was a fake suggestion," Juliette says, but she's smiling, relieved her dad is moving forward with this decision, and others, without her. We're definitely going to college together.

45

ABRAM

It's the weekend after getting back from the beach, and Mom's in the kitchen making breakfast when I walk in searching for a stamp. I find one in her secret candy drawer, slap it on, and slide the envelope toward the pancake griddle so she can see what I'm mailing today.

"Is this what I think it is?" Mom says, pointing the spatula at my college application. I nod, and she wraps her arms around me.

"Just finished filling it out downstairs," I say proudly. "Accepted the tennis scholarship, too."

"Whatever you want to do, Abram, as long as you go to school. And to class while you're there, please—that would be a nice bonus." She turns back to the pancakes and takes a deep breath. "Oh, thank God, I'm so relieved."

"Wow, I must've really looked like I was going nowhere for a while," I say.

"Noooo," Mom says, reaching out and squeezing my

hand. "Well, not since you met the beautiful closet organizer downstairs."

I give her a sheepish grin. "How'd you know she was here already?"

"Moms always know, Abram," she says with a smile. "Plus, she's almost always here."

I find Juliette eavesdropping at the top of the basement stairs.

"Did you hear the part about moms always knowing?" I ask.

"Yes."

"What did you think?"

"I wanted to believe her," she says.

"But?"

She shakes her head. "So I believed her."

Juliette

ABRAM TAKES MY HAND and leads me toward the breakfasty smells escaping from the kitchen. I forgot to bring my appetite, remembered the tension in my neck. I'm leaving as soon as Abram's mom says anything passive-aggressive about our trip to the beach. But I've eavesdropped on enough of her conversations with her son to know she won't; that's just me wanting to go already.

"Mom?" Abram says. Suzy removes several pancakes from the griddle in front of her and turns around. "This is Juliette."

"Hi," I say with a weird wave of my hand. Suzy Morgan

attacks me, all right . . . with a vicious hug! Her body radiates warmth, like Abram's, and I can smell the rosemary-mint conditioner she buys for him in her bouncy blond hair.

"Thank you for coming," she says, sounding genuine. "Next time I promise not to burn the pancakes."

"Oh, no, I'm sure they're fine," I say, looking over at them.

"They're mildly burnt," Abram says by the griddle, picking one up and taking a bite out of it. "Still taste good, though."

"What can I get you to drink?" Suzy asks me. "We have orange juice, milk . . ."

What if I were the kind of Bob Evans farm girl who rubbed her tummy and said, *Mmm, yes, can I have a big, tall glass of milk with a straw, please?*

"Coffee?"

"Yes!" she exclaims. "We have that." As if to prove this is a house of no beverage judgment, Abram reaches into the fridge and pops the tab on a can of Sunkist.

"It's a little on the strong side," Suzy apologizes, handing me a huge casino-branded mug with a red 7-shaped handle. Abram smiles to himself, well aware of my caffeine-glugging tolerance (one of my few high tolerances).

"I'll just sip it," I tell Suzy, because she hasn't stopped caring yet. She smiles and buzzes back to the carafe to pour a cup for herself, too.

The three of us take our seats and start passing plates of food around, salt and pepper shakers, syrup, etc. Suzy's phone blows up several times as her sister, Jane, tries to set her up on a date. Oh, Aunt Jane, whose life I now know better than my own, thanks to Facebook—e.g., her latest post wondering if her feet aching has more to do with the cold weather or her half-marathon training. Thirty-seven people Liked it, practically begging for the next installment, and I was one of them.

True to form, Aunt Jane won't take no for an answer, so eventually Suzy stands up and puts the phone inside the Crock-Pot to slow-cook away any future distractions. I'll have to borrow that recipe from her sometime.

"How do you feel about recently divorced veterinarians?" I ask Suzy when she sits back down. Feeling stupid, I reach under the table for the dog. She's chewing the piece of bacon Abram just gave her. "There's this doctor at the Humane Society, sorry, I shouldn't have—"

Suzy leans forward and smiles. "What's his name?"

I hold up my phone so she can see for herself.

"Now *that's* an option," Suzy says. Abram smiles at me as his mom continues to explore it. I mouth a *Sorry,* he mouths back a *Thank you*.

"I don't think he has any kids," I tell Suzy, thinking that's a huge plus. She looks disappointed for a second, then goes back to staring.

"Okay, enough about my future boyfriend," Suzy says, handing back my phone, "tell me more about the beach. Did you run into Terry and Linda, by any chance?"

Abram and I look at each other, then back at Suzy, who's now looking away. "After I called and asked them to keep an eye on you," she says to the refrigerator.

The three of us share a laugh, splitting it pretty much equally.

ABRAM

JULIETTE AND I put away the dishes while Mom directs Aunt Jane to the Humane Society website over the phone. From the sounds of their conversation, Aunt Jane seems to be approving (we can hear the approval from her end of the line).

"What if he's a creeper?" Juliette whispers, handing me a bowl to place in the dishwasher.

"Then we'll design an exit strategy for her."

"I like where your head's at," she says, "but I'm not sure why you put that bowl there."

"Sorry, baby." I look up and grin, waiting for her brain to reject the "baby." "Too soon?"

"Not at all . . . baby." She can't keep a straight face.

Is this a preview of us two years from now, coexisting in our first crappy on-campus apartment together? I'm thinking so. Ten dollars she won't be scrunching her nose at my pet names by then, either. She'll be like, "Hey, baby, will you stop putting the cookie sheet in the dishwasher when it doesn't fit, please? Or maybe just stop making cookies altogether, babes, thanks?" And I'll say, "I'll take those requests into consideration, sugar cookie." She'll roll her eyes, and then sugar cookie will be her new nickname for a little while, until she goes back to being my baby again.

Juliette's been trying to hand me a plate for a solid ten seconds now.

"My bad, baby."

EPILOGUE

Juliette

THERE SHE IS, standing behind the counter like she's been expecting me. Mindy hasn't changed a bit since she last dispensed my pills, so that's something to appreciate about her. I wore my hair down to surprise Abram today and nearly died from the psychological adjustment on the way over here.

"How are you, Mindy?" I say, sliding my new prescription across the countertop.

She smiles. "I'm well, Juliette. You're looking tanner than I last saw you."

I'm *loving* Mindy these days.

I tell her I was at the beach last week, and she says her boyfriend's parents have a place down that way, OMG, small world. Odd, I've never pictured a boyfriend figure living in Mindy's townhouse—more like a sloppy girl roommate who rolls down the waistband of her baggy sweatpants while making Ramen in the kitchen, a scratched-up dining room table covered in student-loan invoices, and an overfed cat named

Mr. Whiskers who's wondering where it all went wrong. That's my way of expressing that I'm happy Mindy has someone, too.

"Let me just see if we have this medication in stock."

"I think you do," I say. "That was me calling ahead two hours ago."

Nervous laughter from both sides of the counter. It's like some sort of customer-service barrier has been broken, her knowing I call every month, me finally acknowledging it. She comments that it's a lower dosage than I've gotten in the past, and I tell her this will be my last bottle.

While I'm waiting, I walk over to the hair-care aisle to see if she's been restocked. At first I can't find her, start to panic. I remind myself it's okay, that this is just a mind-made form of her, not the real person, which is impossible to capture in an image or the words of anyone else's fuzzy recount, including mine. *Especially* mine. Anyway, I'm still relieved when I find the box. *Hi, Mom. I miss you. You were right about Abram.*

A few minutes later, prescription in hand, I walk out the automatic doors and find him leaning down and petting my dad's early Christmas present: a golden retriever rescue we named Whale. The dog is alternating between looking up at the glowing Redbox screen in front of him, and becoming obsessed with licking off the lotion I applied to Abram's redeveloping tennis calluses earlier. Something's wrong with him. I feel like Whale wants to film the canine version of *Prescription for Love* with Abram's dog and then rent it repeatedly, unable to control himself, just as his crazy dog-mother couldn't. As soon as he's past these tricky teen-dog years, I'll let him make the best decision of his life, at CVS, too.

ABRAM

YEP, I'VE BEEN HERE ALL ALONG, in and out of the store, visiting with Whale the dog, watching my girl be nice to Mindy from the vitamin section. Juliette invited me this time; extended the invitation twenty minutes ago, in my basement. We drove separately, thinking we'd re-create the magical awkwardness of that night we first chatted, but primarily so she could get some solo driving practice. I followed behind her to make sure she did okay, and, hmm, she almost turned left into the wrong lane, accidentally rolling up onto the grassy median that divides the road. She recovered nicely, but she has a ways to go before she's ready to merge onto any highways.

"Ready to go?" she asks.

"Just one second," I say, standing up and digging into my pocket.

It'll be tough to compete with Ben Flynn's early Christmas present, especially when Juliette doesn't want me to get her anything out of fear she'll hate it and accidentally hurt my feelings. Meanwhile, she keeps ordering stuff online with her dad's credit card and having it shipped directly to my basement's sliding door, per the extra-specific instructions on the package. The SHIPPED FROM address is a PO Box, the shipper's name ANONYMOUS, but it's got her Secret Santa signature written all over it. So far, she's gotten me linen sheets for the dorm-room bed she's acting like she won't be spending a lot of time in but really will, and new strings for my racquet with the latest in obnoxious lefty-spin technology. Already played with them at the club a few times, in preparation for my comeback this spring. My dad would've loved them. And he really would've loved the reason why I'm playing again: not because I think it's what he'd want me to do, but because I want to do it.

"You didn't buy me anything, did you?" she asks, as I hide it behind my back.

"It's more of a graduation present than a Christmas gift." The dog is sniffing at my hands, trying to decide whether to eat the remaining lotion or my surprise. I bring it around to show Juliette.

"Big Red," she says, accepting the gum with visible relief. Then she turns the package over and finds the tickets. Two of them, naturally, for a European cruise this summer. Wiped out my mom's Abram's College Gift fund, but the whole cruise aspect was Mom's idea, because she thinks it'll make her worry less about my safety, as well as my tendency to lose important documents.

I put my hands in my pockets, rocking back and forth as I say, "We'll avoid Moscow, check out Paris for a few days, and we're less likely to get mugged in a dark alleyway on a boat."

"My hero."

"Plus, we'll be closer to home."

She nods, knowing I mean the ocean.

"They're refundable, in case you change your mind."

"I'm done changing my mind," she says firmly. Then she smiles, leans forward, and lets me revisit the feeling of her lips on mine, which will never get old, even when we're old, gray whales.